Praise for Dee Tenorio's *Love Me Tomorrow*

"(A) highly enjoyable read."

~ *The Romance Studio*

"(A)n enthralling, nail biting read that will keep you on the edge of your seat. This is book two in Ms. Tenorio's Rancho Del Cielo Romance series, and I'll be heading off to buy the first. Love Me Tomorrow can't wait for tomorrow, it needs to be read today."

~ *Fallen Angels Reviews*

Look for these titles by
Dee Tenorio

Now Available:

Love Me Knots
Test Me

A Rancho Del Cielo Romance
Betting Hearts
Love Me Tomorrow
Burn for Me

The Midnight Trilogy
Midnight Legacy
Midnight Temptation
Midnight Sonata

Love Me Tomorrow

Dee Tenorio

A Samhain Publishing, Ltd. publication.

Samhain Publishing, Ltd.
577 Mulberry Street, Suite 1520
Macon, GA 31201
www.samhainpublishing.com

Love Me Tomorrow

Print ISBN: 978-1-60504-444-6
Digital ISBN: 978-1-60504-375-3

Editing by Deborah Nemeth
Cover by Scott Carpenter

First Samhain Publishing, Ltd. electronic publication: February 2009
First Samhain Publishing, Ltd. print publication: December 2009

Dedication

For Samantha Hunter, who lends an ear, a hand, a heart and a hug as needed. (Even kicks, upon request.)

And for Mauri. Because she's good to me.

Prologue

I stand on the roof of the warehouse, waiting. It's a big bastard. Was probably impressive back when it was shiny and new. Now it just looks like some dented beer can with shit all over it. I'm doing the old man who owns it a favor. He probably won't say as much to the news crews that'll show up, but I can live with the disappointment. I'm getting exactly what I need from it already. It's essential to my plan.

Lighting it was easy. I started with an outlet near the hay stores. It didn't fry the way I expected, but they won't be able to tell. I lit a flare to create the burn marks I need, and let it start the smaller flames. That's all it took. In seconds, they raced into each other, flowing like water over the stacks. The old man will call the fire department in no time.

Until then I can wait alone.

It's nerve wracking, but that's only to be expected. This step is the hardest. After this, there's no turning back. But I don't want to turn back. I want to savor every second of this. I want these next few weeks to last forever.

I want to *feel* the fire eating that man alive.

That's why I'm on the roof. Waiting.

Danny Randall is coming. Rancho del Cielo's famed fire department captain. He always takes the roof first. Everyone loves Danny. Which means it'll hurt that much more when he's gone. Especially for *him.* Nothing stings like regret. He doesn't know it yet, but Josh Whittaker will carry tonight with him for the rest of his life. A scar. The first of many.

Right on time, Randall climbs up the ladder to the roof, axe in hand, already giving directions to the men behind him. They scatter over the tin, their heavy boots keeping them from slipping down the giant slope. Randall comes my way. My jacket and hardhat match Station Fifteen's, but there's no way he can see my face in the dark. I can see him, though, in the glow of his flashlight. His eyes narrow, trying to figure out who I am. Randall knows his team, knows I'm not part of it. Everyone is exactly where they should be, from the three guys up on the roof with him to the ten guys on the grounds below. In his head, he's checking them off, sorting out who has the balls to break formation. None of those obedient bastards would even think about it. They don't have the vision I do. They can't see a second beyond their own pathetic lives, neat in their tiny boxes of mediocrity. I bet they couldn't make a decision on their own if their lives depended on it. But they'll have to, soon enough.

I can see the heat on Randall's face. His hair pokes down his forehead, already matting down on his skin. The place is way beyond saving, but the town golden boy thinks he's gonna give it a try anyway. Randall walks closer. I can't help smiling a little. It's like it doesn't even occur to him to wonder if he's in danger. And he is. Just another step or two...

But Randall stops. "You're not on my shift."

Should I answer the obvious? The others will never hear.

"Who are you?" Randall yells, taking another step.

"No one," I yell back.

Randall starts working his teeth back and forth. I'm pissing him off. Good. He takes another step, the final step, and the roof gives way beneath him.

If it wasn't for the axe, he would have fallen the fifty feet to his instantaneous death, but Randall has quick reflexes. The edge of the axe lodges in the tin, leaving him dangling with a one-handed grip to the long handle.

Bad luck. I didn't want to do it this way. He was supposed to fall. It was supposed to look like the weakened roof dropped him like a stone. Quick. Painless. Just because I need him dead doesn't mean he has to feel pain or fear. It's not his fault he's my target. Nothing for it now.

I crouch down around the edge of the jagged hole and put my gloved hands around the head of the axe. It skids with a shriek on the metal.

"Since you won't be around much longer, I might as well tell you."

Randall can see me now, thanks to the firelight from below. His mouth falls slack. But not his grip.

I smile at him. "This is revenge. Pure and simple. In a matter of months, everything Josh Whittaker has ever cared about—you, his sister, his *girlfriend...*"

Randall's eyes go wide, panic finally entering them. I figured it would.

"You'll all be gone." Time is short. Someone is going to notice or hear in a second. I shove at the axe again while he grapples for leverage, yelling for someone to come. "I'm going to let him live his life in misery. Just like I have. But you..." I shove, hard. "You get to die wondering why."

The axe finally tears through the metal and I watch his fall to the concrete and boxes at the bottom. It's not like they show in movies, all slow and quiet. Death never is. It's fast, like dropping a rock down a well. Impossible to take back. Randall screams, still reaching out for me. I can't tell if he's angry or afraid. It doesn't matter. He hits the ground and it hits him back. I can't see his eyes from here, but I know he's dead.

I stare down, even as others start to scramble. I want to memorize the sight of his broken body beneath me. Use it to replace my first memory of fire. Of blood. My first reward for years of pain. For every loss Josh Whittaker caused. Losses he'll spend the rest of his life paying for.

ঙ৪ঌ

Something big fell from the ceiling.

At first, Josh thought it was a beam. Some part of the tin roof. But the corner of his peripheral vision registered the yellow slicker. Then he heard it, over the building roar of the flames—a man's scream of horror.

The sound of the body hitting the ground was a sick thud he knew would never be erased from his memory.

He ran toward it, pushing past burning crates, past other firefighters, tearing at his mask to see better. Even without it, disbelief clawed at him. From the thick blonde hair, freed by the fallen hardhat, it could only be Danny. But it couldn't be. It couldn't.

On his knees, Josh tried to find a way to staunch the flow of blood. Only it flowed from everywhere. Bones tented the reinforced fabric of Danny's gear where his thigh should be, his foot pointing in a grotesque direction. The other twisted like that of a broken doll. Josh gauged the fall, his stomach clenching at the distance because the clinical part of his mind knew there was no surviving it. Most of the bones had to be broken like those in Danny's legs, but the majority of the blood was coming from his head. The back of his skull was no doubt crushed. But then Danny made a sound. A gurgle of agony.

Josh lowered his head, oblivious to the flames surrounding

them, desperate to hear. Danny sputtered blood in his attempt to form the word. His eyes glazed, staring sightlessly upward as his last breath pushed out the trailing end of the word. The name. *Miranda.*

Then he was gone.

"No," Josh whispered, looking for some place to touch that wasn't already damaged to drag Danny back by, but there wasn't anywhere. Finally, he pounded on Danny's chest, swearing and forcing himself to use CPR techniques he'd ingrained so deep they were second nature, without response. "God damn it, Danny, don't you die. Wake up, Danny. Do you hear me? Wake up!"

He kept pushing, kept fighting, knowing inside that nothing could be done. Nothing ever could. But Danny's last word scorched something in him and he couldn't stop. Wouldn't stop. The others came, dragging him away so they could lift the broken body and carry it through the flames, no doubt thinking it was love for his friend, for his brother, that had driven him.

It wasn't until the next day, long after he'd announced he needed a few days off and he wanted to be left completely alone, that he allowed himself to admit that it wasn't. The man he would have easily died for, who he had barely spoken a word to in the last six months that wasn't a required reply to an order, deserved more. Instead, Danny was the man whose last word had made Josh want to hurt him even more.

And there wasn't a damn thing he could do about it.

Chapter One

"Oh, hell." Josh might have stood a chance at avoiding the slim redhead on his front porch if he had seen her hand on the threshold before he slammed the heavy oak door on it.

But he doubted it.

At Miranda McTiernan's loud yelp of agony, cold sobriety cleared his mind and age-old reflexes sprang him back to the door. She stood there, cradling her hand and swearing for all she was worth. Though he would never admit it, he was impressed with the assortment of curses in her arsenal. It had grown since the last time she'd unleashed it on him.

"Lemme guess." She winced and stamped her foot, clamping her upper lip with her teeth. "Bad hangover?" Good old Randa. She could be hanging onto a severed limb and still not let an opportunity for sarcasm to slip by.

He scrubbed his hand over his unshaved jaw. "No."

She raised a brow.

"I wasn't done being drunk yet." He reached for her cradled palm, groaning inwardly when she wordlessly allowed him to take it. She had to be in pain. She did nothing without words. Lots and lots of words.

He should have expected her. Everyone else in town—even a place as nosy as Rancho del Cielo—knew to leave him alone in his grief. Not Miranda. She'd never heard of the word *boundaries.*

He pulled her inside, this time closing the door slow. She moved as if she were brittle. Or whole-body sore. Her color wasn't any good, either. She hadn't been at her best these last several months, the strain between them taking its toll, but that was nothing compared to now. Her skin looked papery, stretched tight over her cheekbones with stress. Her eyes were swollen, bloodshot, something he could see she'd tried to hide with eyeliner. The shadows under them looked like deep bruises beneath the pale white stuff she'd spread on to camouflage them.

Danny was her friend too, he reminded himself, the urge to pull her into his arms and let her cry so strong his hands actually lifted.

He was more *than her friend,* a darker part of himself interrupted. His hands fell to his sides. Grumbling, he led her toward the back of his home where the kitchen—and his first-aid kit—awaited. They sat at his dinette table, her hand between them.

The damage was worse than he expected. The top of her hand was scraped, leaving only the rolled-up strings of dead skin. It had a raw, angry look to it, spots of blood forming here and there. Guilt knifed in his gut, sharp and unforgiving. One more infraction to add to his long list of wrongs where she was concerned. He pressed gingerly on each finger, checking for any breaks. When he didn't find one, he began cleaning and salving. They remained silent while he worked. Except for a slight gasp here and there, Miranda didn't react to his ministrations.

Definitely worrisome.

When he finished, he looked into eyes that usually held challenge in them. Instead, he found concern.

It burned in his belly. “You shouldn’t have come.” To his own ears, his voice rumbled with anger.

She looked away. “I had to.”

She would think that. If they had lost anyone else, he might have been grateful for the company. In ways he didn’t like admitting, Miranda always knew how to make him feel better. Could draw him out and make the worst things seem incidental or at least not as bad as they’d seemed. But this was Danny. She was the last person who could bring him any comfort from this.

“I’m fine.” He closed the kit, wanting to slam it, careful to click the lid into place in near silence. Her presence made the loss too real. He’d been drinking so he wouldn’t have to think about Danny—the loss or the mess between all three of them. Things should be different, damn it. Now nothing could be made right, and looking at her only drove the point home.

She nodded too wearily to have believed him. And probably said nothing because she knew it would just lead to another argument that wasn’t about the real issue. They were good at that.

He should have known better than to have tried to fool her. He also should have felt guilty, but he had enough on his plate already.

“There was something else I need to talk to you about. Something that can’t wait.”

What could possibly be so important that it broke her from her mourning? At first nothing struck him as likely. But then he remembered who he was dealing with. He didn’t want to deal with this right now. He didn’t want to deal with anything. He wanted to be selfish and just blank out until the pain went away.

That wasn’t how this particular redhead did things,

though. Few people in the world needed help quite like Miranda. The higher her stress, the more likely she'd call him. Oh, she claimed she did things for his own good when she could get away with it, but he could see the tension in the set of her jaw. Losing Danny was ripping her up—she probably just didn't want to be alone. Hello unnecessary visit.

What would it be this time? Had her idiot dog, Rusty, knocked up some unsuspecting thoroughbred again? Or was a wall falling down in her precious house again? With Miranda, he could never quite be sure. But hell if he was asking this time. He waited until she lifted her lashes, her bright green eyes a sudden punch to the gut he didn't need. Why did he have the feeling this wasn't going to be a typical Miranda request?

She pushed out a breath and spoke, but he couldn't make out the words.

He squinted. He should ask. He should, but he wouldn't. If he didn't hear her, he couldn't be held responsible for her actions.

Finally she scrunched her face, frustrated. "A *baby*, Josh. I'm here because I need you to give me a baby."

He stared blankly at her. "From where?" No one would be dumb enough to ask *him* to babysit. Least of all right now.

"Um..." Her cheeks flushed, that bright red shade she claimed made her look "swollen" instead of "up to something". Her gaze skittered to the side. "That's not how I meant."

Then what did she mean?

"I want *your* baby."

He'd have choked if he could manage to breathe. Any second now she was going to start laughing and tell him she'd been trying to shock a response out of him, so he wouldn't automatically say no to what she really wanted.

She didn't say anything.

Maybe she was waiting for him to turn her favorite tinge of purple? But the longer he stayed quiet, the more miserable she got.

Good God, she was serious.

"I need more liquor." He reached blindly toward his refrigerator, almost knocking his chair over in his haste. He'd stocked up specifically for this day, but looking at the fourteen brown bottles left on the top shelf, he wasn't sure he had enough. It would have to do. Within moments, he had a cold beer in his hands. One look at her mortified face, though, and he was unable to drink it. He put it back in the fridge and slammed the door.

He tried to fathom what could have been going through her head, but he'd learned years ago that it was impossible to understand her circuitous mind. He ran both hands through his hair, pulling a little so he wouldn't give into the need to leave the room and pretend she'd never come over. "Couldn't you have asked me this when I was still drunk?"

"Believe me, it crossed my mind." Her smile might be wry, but he knew her well enough to know she wasn't kidding. He was lucky he hadn't woken up from a drunken stupor with her already in his bed. "I know it's a lot to ask—"

"You're damn right it is." Too much, especially considering their history—God, considering the fact that her former fiancé wasn't even cold. "Why are you coming to me?"

His pounding head throbbed at the question that immediately came to mind next. What would he have done if she'd gone to anyone else?

It didn't bear thinking about.

She opened her mouth, her answer so ready there was no way it wasn't rehearsed to get under his skin.

"Never mind. Don't answer that. Isn't this something you should talk to Trisha or Penelope about? You know, girl stuff?" He felt a gush of relief just thinking about off-loading this problem onto his sister or their other best friend. Hell, Penelope was Miranda's doctor. She was *supposed* to deal with this.

"God, no, I couldn't talk to Trisha. I couldn't handle her pity."

Even with a rampaging headache on the rise, he couldn't miss that cue. This was no run-of-the-mill Miranda problem. He looked her up and down but nothing stood out other than the markers of her grief. No wrinkles on her black pantsuit. No tangles in her Shirley-Temple hair. No broken bones, burns, blood or signs of serious illness. "What's pity got to do with it?"

"I don't want *your* pity, either." She pointed with her good hand at him.

He put up his palms in a helpless gesture.

She sighed, dropping her head. He could only see the top of her mop of red curls. Curls he used to pull mercilessly when they were growing up. He still remembered how glossy they felt the other times he'd touched them. Around his fingers, against his lips...

"I'm sorry." Her voice thankfully yanked him away from unwelcome memories. "I...this isn't easy for me."

"Just spit it out. We'll both feel better." Well, he would. Especially after she left. Without anything resembling a baby.

"Give me a second, okay?"

"Miranda." He forced himself to feign patience. If he didn't, she'd balk and he'd never find out what the hell she was up to. Which meant he'd never find a way to derail her. "Explain already. I promise I won't get mad."

Famous last words.

She lifted her head and if the flash of intuition that had served him well all his life hadn't spoken, he'd still have wished the words back. All he could do now was wait for her to stop thinking and start talking. And hope the impact wouldn't stagger him.

Miranda stood up and headed for the coffeemaker. Moving kept her from cracking under the pressure in Josh's bright blue eyes. She wasn't in his house as often as she'd been as a kid, but in the years since his mother and stepfather had relocated to Florida, Josh hadn't changed many of the basics. Wallpaper, carpets, cosmetic stuff, yes. Appliances? Not a chance in hell. As if he thought he wouldn't be able to figure out a machine built after the year two thousand. Soon enough, the ancient machine was bubbling and burping, giving a knock or two as it boiled. Eventually, something dark spewed into the pot and rather than ponder what else it likely was, she opted to accept it as coffee and filled two mugs she'd gathered while waiting.

If Josh weren't watching her nervous activity, she probably would have gathered all the dishes from the various places on the counters and loaded the dishwasher. But he knew all her cues and she forced herself only to clear enough of a spot to work. Even trying to outthink him was better than actually having the conversation she was planning.

You can always forget it, her conscience reminded her again, but like all the other times, it was a lie. She wouldn't forget. And more years would go to waste. Maybe all of her along with them.

She offered him one of the mugs and they sat in amiable silence while each drank. She purposely ignored the way he kept his gaze trained on her over the rim of his mug. Then she traced the scratches in the wooden table. Finally he took the decision out of her hands.

"What's wrong, Miranda?"

Now or never, Red. It's what Danny used to tell her every time she had to put up or shut up, especially when it came to Josh. Danny always figured out her plans pretty quick—he generally just liked to see if she had the stones to pull them off. He'd be laughing his ass off right about now. It seemed wrong that he wasn't here to do it. But if he were, would she have had the courage to come?

No.

The answer cemented her decision. She set her cup down. When she met his gaze this time, all her self-doubt was gone. "I'm running out of time to have children."

He rolled his eyes. "For the love of God, you're thirty-one. You have plenty of time."

She suppressed the urge to smack him. "Oh? And who told you that? The fertility fairy?"

He blinked, his brows coming together in a crash as he realized what she was saying.

"Not everyone can afford to take biology for granted."

"I'm sorry, Rand." Sincerity, while he stared down at the depths of his mug. It lacked the sympathy anyone else would have given, but she didn't doubt him. She might not like what he said most of the time, but he never said anything he didn't mean.

"Yeah," she sighed. Part of her still wished he could express his emotions while looking her in the eye. But this was Josh. Expressing his emotions never went well in the first place. "I'm sorry, too."

He must have understood that her regrets meant more than her inability to have children. The intensity of his gaze was a stark reminder of all they'd never had. What he'd never *allowed* them to have.

"I have the money I need to do the procedures that are likely to work," she continued, "but I'm uncomfortable with the idea of sperm banks. I wouldn't know anything important about the father. Nothing real, anyway. My baby wouldn't have any history and that sounds horrible to me. I'm being selfish enough as it is, trying to have a baby alone. I want this child to have two parents, to know its family. The best one I could possibly give it." The only one. Her parents had died more than a decade ago. But Josh's mother, Billie, was already an incredible grandmother to Trisha's three kids. Trisha herself loved anything with dimples. They would be perfect.

"Much as I appreciate your affection for my family, you're forgetting a big detail," Josh reminded her, poking into her plans the way he always did.

She met his gaze, unperturbed. "What's that?"

"Me."

Miranda frowned. "I don't think so. You're kind of integral to the plan."

His right eye squinted at the corner. "You'd be dealing with *me*, Randa. Not my mother. Not my sister. Me. And all we do is fight."

As if he didn't know why. "Don't exaggerate."

"I don't have to. Just ask anyone at Jimmy's Grocery."

Against her will, she blushed again. They'd made complete fools out of themselves by fighting in public. The clearest part of that argument was the end. When all was said and done, the aisle had been covered in spaghetti sauce, toilet paper, corn flakes, milk and Josh had a steak lying awkwardly on the top of his head. She could still hear the juicy splat in her head whenever she thought about it.

"We've both matured since then. Look at us right now."

He didn't budge. "We haven't grown up that much in the last six months." Thankfully, he didn't mention this was the longest calm conversation they'd had in the last six months, too. "You can't really think this is the kind of relationship to bring a child into."

Josh-rational-speak for "no".

In the face of that, she was going to have to club him with some reality. "You're all I have." She opted not to remind him exactly why. "What's the likelihood that I'll meet Mr. Perfect and convince him to have a baby with me before my time is up?"

His mouth curved into a smug grin. "Are you implying that I'm Mr. Perfect?"

Okay then, maybe she did have to remind him. "No, you're Mr. Overbearing-jerk-who-intimidates-any-man-who-comes-near-me. I'm in a time crunch."

She practically heard the clank of his smile dropping. "You aren't scoring any points, Ace."

"I'm trying to be honest and straightforward."

Ha! her conscience accused loudly. Miranda ignored it.

Josh stared at her for endless seconds. Then he shook his head, his dark hair catching the light. "Then there's the other thing."

She let the silence stretch between them. The *other* thing. The thing he never wanted to talk about but always somehow seemed to remember when it suited him. Her greatest moment of weakness. The one time she'd allowed hopelessness to swallow her, and while he never said a word directly about it, she knew he'd never quite forgiven her for it. And now he wanted to use it as an excuse. "What other thing?"

"You know." Yes, she'd been able to tell just by the

disapproving downward cast to his lips, as usual. As if it left a bad taste in his mouth just to think about.

At least he didn't have to know the flavor of regret. "That was twelve years ago, Josh. I'm not the same person I was back then."

"When people go that far, it's a testament to the strength of their character."

"Now you're judging my character?" Her disbelief rang in her ears.

"No. And don't look at me that way. You know I think you're one of the funniest, best people in the world."

On any other day, she'd have been moved to hear him say something like that. However, the giant, dangling *but* kind of ruined the moment.

"But a child pushes people to their limits. Sometimes beyond their limits." He took another drink. Like she didn't know who he was talking about. She was hardly like his father, and the fact that he could calmly compare her to a man he couldn't even bring himself to name on most occasions did more than gall. He didn't even seem to realize how insulting he'd just been. It'd serve him right if she threw her half-full mug at his head. But no. He just sat there, content to leave the insult shadowed in thoughtful ambiguity.

She wasn't. "If I didn't know better, I'd think you just said it's for the best if I don't have children."

His blue eyes widened, stark with surprise. But he didn't say anything to take it back.

She felt the silence like a blow to the chest. "Wow." She didn't know what else to say. Words came to mind, awful, accusing words she wanted to fling at him in hurt, but all she pushed through her lips was another shocked, "Wow."

"Try to see this from my point of view—"

Bitter laughter overflowed. "As if *you* had a clue how to do that."

His mouth quirked but he brushed off her remark with a half-shrug.

"I mean, I'm not an idiot." Much as he liked to think she was. "I knew you'd freak out. That we'd have to talk about it a lot before you even considered helping me but...wow, Josh. Even for you, that was low."

His brows crashed together. "What do you mean, *even for me*?"

She ignored him. "I was a kid. Alone. I'd just lost everything and everyone that ever meant anything to me."

His face remained impassive. Heaven forbid he acknowledge his part in that particular statement.

"I never expect you to forgive me, but God, I at least thought you understood why."

He finally looked away.

Her lips flattened into a hard line. Trisha always warned her to stop hoping for miracles with Josh. Even Danny had told her they were hopeless dreams. But still, she'd gone on with her fantasies about knowing him better than he knew himself. Kept thinking that if she just drew him a line from point *A* to point *B*, he'd figure out the way things were supposed to be. She'd gotten herself all the way to point *Z* and he wasn't budging off the starting block. "I guess I really do expect too much of you."

His gaze slanted her way with the precision of a laser, coolly blue. "You can't blame me for taking it into consideration. I notice you're not talking adopting. Does that mean Social Services considered the fact that you once tried to kill yourself too?"

Miranda stood up slowly, making sure he could see it wasn't a fit of anger or an impulsive act. She kept their gazes connected. The better for him to see her disdain. When she turned away, it was to leave.

His hand snaked out to grab hers. "Don't hold this against me, Rand."

She stared down at his hand, but he didn't let go. Of course he didn't. He could throw around the judgment, but he never could quite free her. She pried out of his grip. "Why would I? I'm not the one who punishes people with grudges here, am I?"

"Dammit, this is not about a grudge!" Now he was on his feet.

She made for the front door. "Tell yourself that if it makes you feel any better."

He caught her again, spinning her around. "I am not punishing you."

Sure he wasn't. Miranda raised her chin. She knew every line on his face. Knew every scar. Every expression. He glowered down at her, indignant because he really thought he was telling the truth. The longer she stayed silent, the more his anger softened to remorse. Warmth he could never completely erase filled his eyes. It was that warmth that always gave her hope, no matter what came out of his mouth.

His grip loosened, his fingers gently running down her arm. He took hold of her hand. Her heart slowed, the desire to forgive him as strong as every other feeling she had for him. But he wasn't going to change his mind about anything if she melted every time he gave her a puppy dog look. And his being blind wasn't an excuse to hurt the people he loved.

"Are you coming to the funeral?"

His eyes lost any regrets or warmth. He let go as if she were poison. "No."

"Josh—"

"*Don't.*"

Eyes stinging sharper than before, she nodded and walked to the door. She tried not to flinch when it slammed behind her.

Chapter Two

Josh didn't have it in him to get drunk again after Miranda's strange visit. It had taken too much resolve to get drunk the first time.

Inebriated or not, the next two weeks passed in a blur. Each day leading up to Danny's procession strung his nerves ever tighter. If it hadn't taken so long to arrange, he sometimes wondered, would it have bothered him as much? Or was it just Miranda's accusation making him run circles in his head? There was no way of knowing. When the day finally came, he spent it out at the lake, where he and Danny had spent most of their free time together as adults, watching the rippling surface and waiting for some kind of peace to take root in him.

Hours went by, but it didn't happen. He couldn't let go. He wanted to. He'd give anything not to be angry anymore. Danny was the one who'd seen him at his best and his worst, who knew all those secrets everyone wished they didn't have. He should be destroyed inside. He should be crying, waving his fist at God, demanding to know why. Anything but feeling this anger. It was stupid to be angry at a dead man. Stupid and pointless. But it felt as if his pain was the only thing of Danny left, and he couldn't make himself release it. He held it tighter, halfheartedly daring his friend to try to take it way.

Yeah? Me and what army? Josh could almost hear Danny's

voice, a whisper that was probably more memory than imagination. *I'm not taking those odds, buddy.*

"You could give it a shot," Josh said to the wind, the only thing out on the lake to hear him.

It blew around him, a welcome cool touch to the summer sun. But it didn't answer.

"You're not gonna believe what Miranda's come up with this time," he said, louder. He even laughed, though it felt hollow. "She wants kids. With *me*. Can you even picture that?"

Danny probably would have had no trouble at all with the mental image. He'd talk about how happy Miranda would be while Josh would be sweating out details like college tuitions and the cost of a car in sixteen years. Danny was dumb like that, though Josh never really put it in those words. But then Danny didn't understand that being responsible for someone's life didn't stop when the fire was out and the helmets were off. He'd always said Josh should relax more, trust Miranda to figure things out on her own. Show a little faith, he'd said over and over. The same way he'd said not to worry when Trisha married her Michael. Ten years and three kids later, he still worried. And Trisha didn't even have the energy to get into trouble anymore. But she used to. When she and Miranda were little it was all he could do to keep them in one piece.

The memory blindsided him as fast as his father's hand.

"Why weren't you watching her?" The blow landed so fast Josh hit the side of the doorway before he'd even realized his father had struck.

"Jared!" His mother had yelled, but she kept her place on her knees by the dining room table, tweezers in hand. Trisha sat on the chair, tear-stained cheeks red, eyes wide. Only four, but she knew better than to say anything already. She'd learned faster than Josh had. "He wasn't even here, damn it! *I* was watching her."

Josh righted himself, slipping his backpack off his shoulder. Trisha's arm trembled on her lap, not from fear but what had to be pain. A long scrape bled from the back of her hand up to her elbow, red and angry with bits of skin peeled back and splinters of all sizes sticking out. It looked like it hurt, but Trisha kept her eyes on their father's angry pacing.

"What the hell were you doing, then, Billie? Talking on the phone with one of your fuckin' friends? Look at her! Bleeding all over the goddamned place. How many times have I told the you to stay out of that tree house? How many?" Jared could spin his rages on a dime. No one was ever safe when he got like that.

Josh tried not to react when Trisha's panicked eyes turned his way as she braced for Jared to grab her. The tree house had fallen down last summer, but stayed mostly intact. He and Danny liked to sneak in there still to get away from the girls. His father kept threatening to break it into kindling, but all year it had sat there like a pile of forgotten leaves, growing moss and mold and becoming a six-year-old boy's paradise. He and Danny never got caught in there, but Trisha hadn't mastered sneakiness yet. She'd been yelled at twice. Two times more than Jared would have given Josh to learn anything.

It was too much to hope their father wouldn't pick up on her silent plea for him to intervene. Jared's head turned, his face a mask of anger and some sick satisfaction he always seemed to get when he could blame things on Josh. Like it made him happy or something. "It was you, you little shit, wasn't it? You're the one going in there and making her think it's all right not to listen to me."

Josh's arm yanked his whole body all the way into his father's leg. Then he felt the clamp of Jared's hand around his wrist and realized he'd been dragged over. His shoulder ached where it had jolted.

"You see what you did to your sister?" Another full body shake forward. "Look! She's bleeding because of you and your stupid friend. No one is supposed to be in that tree house. Do you hear me this time, Josh? Are you listening? No one!" Josh felt himself rattle to the side. "You're gonna hear me now, though, boy."

Trisha had started crying again, this time loudly. She always cried when Jared started in on him, never seemed to figure out it just made the jerk angrier.

Josh waited for the sound of the belt coming free but all he felt was the hard brush of his father's workpants against his arm and face as the man passed him by. The three of them stayed in the dining room, Billie quietly continuing to clean the angry scrape, Trisha crying into her shirt and he, still scrunched into his shoulders, waiting for his father to come back. They listened to the sound of chopping wood and swearing, the destruction of the tree house finally complete in the backyard.

Long minutes later, Jared stomped through the house, stopping only to grab his jacket and slam out the door, yelling over his shoulder that he wanted the shit in the backyard cleaned up before he came home. No one had taken a deep breath until the sound of the engine had faded down the street.

Just another fabulous day in the Whittaker house.

Josh swore at himself for even allowing himself to remember. He'd come here to think about *Danny*, not reminisce over useless crap like his father. To try to say goodbye to his friend. He hadn't wanted to do it in a crowd, everyone watching to see if he meant it when he offered his condolences to the Randalls. They didn't need it and he couldn't take it. But that plan didn't work either.

Instead of remembering the boy he'd grown up with, the friend he'd trusted with most everything than meant anything to him…all he could see was the man who'd betrayed him, flaws in a stranger he didn't want to know. The broken, lifeless body he hadn't been able to save. Anger only brewed worse.

The breeze wrapped around him, but forgiveness didn't beckon. Not from within, certainly not from without.

Frustrated, he headed for home with barely enough time to get there before his other longtime friend, Raul Montenga, was supposed to arrive. Raul had said he'd be by after the reception. Except it wasn't Raul he found waiting. Miranda's car was parked in front of his house.

He hadn't seen her since her visit. Which worked out because she was the last person he wanted to deal with. But, he accepted, she also had the singular capability of removing him from all reason at the drop of a hat. The way he felt now, that talent could come in handy. Plus, she and Raul had always gotten on like a house on fire. With the two of them distracting him, he just might not think about the fact that they'd put the best man any of them had ever known in the ground today.

Bone weary, he parked his truck and walked into his own house. She responded right away when he called her name, luring him toward the back yard. A slight breeze wandered in through the open windows along with soft music from the patio. Before, Miranda was the one who used to water his plants and pick up the mail when he was on duty. It had been their arrangement so she could have open access to his pool. When everything went to hell last year, it hadn't occurred to him to ask for his key back. Or return the one she'd traded, come to think of it. That was still hanging on his key ring.

It never struck him as a big problem until he got to the window and saw what she was wearing. There was so little of it, he was unsure if he could call it a bathing suit. All he could do was stand and stare.

It wasn't that he was stupid—he knew Miranda still had a good figure. Hell, his friends had drooled over her for years. He waged a constant war with himself not to see her that way and for the most part succeeded. But, Good Lord in Heaven, he didn't know the woman could cause brain damage.

To think he'd teased her about her jogging and workouts. Every inch of her was firm—tight, even. Her red curls were scraped back into an unforgiving ponytail, leaving the ivory sculpture of her face exposed. Those green eyes glittered bright in the late afternoon light. Her pixyish features flaunted a seductive quality he'd never seen in her before. The tiny black bikini brought to his attention other things he hadn't noticed in years. Not on purpose, anyway.

Her full breasts were pushed up—almost out—just for his inspection. Creamy skin graced the ribcage that narrowed to her slim waist. The minute suit bottom had thin black strings tied just above her curved hips, strings he just knew would untie and fall off as soon as she hit the water. He spent what felt like whole minutes eyeing her long legs. The lean thighs, particularly the keyhole space where they almost touched the fabric of her suit bottom. The strong muscles that curved toward her knees and flared out to slim calves. He followed the line right down to her small ankles, smooth feet and perfect red pedicure.

Safe behind the window, he let his imagination wander to places he hadn't gone in a decade. Remembered textures, scents and sounds filled his mind as he considered each individual part of her body. The flavor of her heartbeat. The warmth of her breath. The liquid welcome as she'd drawn him home... His hands itched to touch, his mouth watered to taste and dammit, his jeans failed to loosen.

She dove into the pool, sliding into the water—and his delusions—with hardly a splash. When she climbed out again, pulling herself up with the help of the handlebars in the deep end, he totally lost his ability to think.

He pushed through the screen door to get closer.

She dripped water, her eyelashes carrying droplets and her mouth curved into a smile trained directly on him. Josh had a hard time pulling in a deep enough breath. Until some part of his brain not rendered stupid noticed something out of sync. It wasn't her usual smile. The one that brightened her whole face and whole parts of his life. No, this one was confident. Pleased. Self-satisfied.

Son of a bitch.

"Hey, Josh. I needed a swim, hope you don't mind."

Hairs on the back of his neck rose and tingled at the husky tone of her voice. *Careful. Don't let her know you're on to her—whatever it was she was doing.* Thankfully for his blood-deprived mind, it wasn't hard to guess what that might be. "Nope. My casa is your casa, right?"

Her smile widened and she sauntered out to the lawn chair beneath the large patio umbrella. She lay below its shade, hiding from the direct beams of the sun, even though it was sinking behind the hills. She had to. Everyone in town knew she burned like a witch in Salem under direct sunlight. Anyone with a brain would know cream-colored skin like hers didn't need sun anyway.

But he wasn't supposed to have a brain right now.

So he watched her brush off all the excess water. Her fingers almost seemed to be caressing her own skin, over her forearms up to her shoulders, down her curved neck. He almost forgot how important breathing was when she ran her fingers over the slope of her half-exposed breast.

"Can you bring me a beer?"

She hated beer and he knew it, but that didn't register right away.

By the time it did, he'd already turned back into the kitchen and grabbed two from the fridge. He almost said something right then, but she turned to him with a diabetes-inducing smile. The little brat thought she had him exactly where she wanted, didn't she?

"Josh?" She pulled a small bottle of lotion from her tiny terrycloth robe and started applying it to her arms and chest.

He watched, unable to decide which of them to be more disgusted with. Her for thinking he'd fall for this stupid plan to seduce him or himself for being dumb enough to almost prove her right. At her humming, he shook his head and sighed. She was moving so damn slow, the sun would be down before she ever got it applied everywhere it needed to be. Oh, yeah, Miranda definitely needed a shakeup.

"I haven't seen that suit yet. Is it new?" he asked, handing her the beer, purposely keeping the entranced puppy look on his face. When her fingertips slid between her breasts, it took considerably less effort to do.

"Yup. It showed the most skin. It's not very me, but I need an allover tan."

He frowned, accidentally losing his stunned-stupid gaze. "What for?"

"Because men like tans. You turned me down. Now I have to attract someone else to be a father. I figure it'll help."

He screwed his brows together in consternation. "I thought you wanted the best family you knew for your baby." Hadn't she mentioned something about that when she was prattling about sperm donors? His eyes followed her oiled hands across her skin without his permission. How much lotion did two breasts really need?

Finally, she had mercy and moved on. The problem was that she reached around her ribs one side at a time, her inner elbows pushing the outer sides of her breasts inward so that the shining flesh pressed together and lifted upward and his brain began to throb. She arched her back and ran one palm down her smooth belly in a way that had his throat closing up. God help him if those searching fingers were going where he thought they were.

Instead, just as she touched the edge of that skimpy bikini line, she lowered her hips and strangely, his lungs deflated as if he'd been holding his breath.

"I did, but your family isn't available." She actually stopped to blink over at him with a saccharine grin. "Truth is, I don't have to be so picky. We live in RDC. I've known just about every man here all my life. I know *everyone's* family. There's plenty of men to pick from."

His breath stopped moving for entirely new reasons. She'd better not be thinking what he thought she was thinking. "You don't really believe you can just talk someone into fathering a child for you?"

She gave a spurt of disbelief. "Are you kidding? No one is going to volunteer for that. Not with you constantly browbeating anyone who looks at me."

He almost let himself sigh, relieved.

"So I've decided to become promiscuous. If I'm easy enough, no one will think about you at all." She had the audacity to wink.

Do not choke.

"You've gotta admit, it's the one thing I haven't tried. Even you can't beat up every man in town."

Do. Not. Choke. Her.

He scratched the side of his head so hard it was likely bleeding. "Aren't you overestimating here? I mean, not that you couldn't get their attention, but there aren't many available men just wandering around RDC, waiting for a promiscuous woman to fall into their laps."

She stared at him incredulously, but he continued calculating which men in their tiny little town she had to choose from. Thankfully for his escalating blood pressure, pickings were slim. He knew most men close to their ages were married or just damn ugly. Except for the guys at the—

"What about the guys at the firehouse? I'm sure a few of them wouldn't mind a tumble. What about Andy Raymond? He likes me. He probably wouldn't turn me down if we went out on a date."

Of course Andy wouldn't. The kid left a trail of drool behind her whenever she was in the station. Josh's brain skidded to a halt as he tried to think of a good way to deter her.

"No." It was all that came to mind.

She turned innocent eyes on him. Some feat, considering that Miranda was the least innocent person he knew.

"Why not?"

"Why not? Why not?" Shit. Back to square one. "The gossips," he finally dragged out of his ass.

RDC did only two things well. Go over a hundred degrees in the summer and gossip. Mae Belle Butner and her band of regulars over at "Shaky Jake's"—a bar and restaurant that might as well be the town meeting hall—would have the entire town talking the second she stepped out on her date. Hell, they'd know she was pregnant before Miranda did.

"You think your baby would be able to live down your

reputation after something like that?" Heartened by her blank blink, he picked up steam. "You know what this place is like. People are going to find out no matter what you do. Talk and *bet.*" Had she forgotten Luke Wilson's wedding already? Because, despite the two years since, no one else had. Especially not the wild rounds of betting that surrounded it.

Her mouth quirked to one side. "I can afford to move."

Of course she could. Her illustrated children's books had been doing well for more than a few years. There was even merchandise starting to stream into stores. She could afford whatever she damn well wanted. But the thought of her leaving left him even colder than the prospect of her traipsing around with any guy she could find. He searched for another tack.

"You can't leave your house. You love that house." It was falling down around her ears because she refused to update it to safety code, but she loved it.

"I don't have to sell it. I'll figure that part out later."

She continued rubbing the coconut-smelling concoction over her legs, lifting them straight up, one at a time, all but purring at the touch of her own hands. Josh scrambled for something else to think about other than her apparent flexibility.

"Well, it can't be Andy, he's only twenty-two."

"Young is good." She smiled lasciviously, eyes closed while she sighed, dropping her forehead to press against her shin, wearing a slow grin he could only call sinful. "I like a guy with…energy."

He couldn't contain a convulsion.

"Besides, it's not as if I'm limited to just Rancho del Cielo. We're not exactly in quarantine here. There's available men in San Diego. Even Orange County if I want. I could sleep with any number of them."

"You can't go around having unprotected sex with people until you get pregnant! It's stupid and it's dangerous!" Trump card. It was one thing to let Miranda get away with manipulating him. It was something else to let her get into that kind of trouble with other men. She'd behave now, he was sure.

Except she looked like he'd just stolen her bunny. She lowered her leg and any trace of a smile melted away. Suddenly, she seemed so uncertain and almost afraid, he wanted to scoop her into his arms and just hold her for a while.

Which would lead in all the wrong directions. He had to make sure she understood, and comforting her wasn't the way to go about it.

"I guess you're right," she conceded. "It's not the same world out there as it was when we were kids. It wouldn't be safe." She took a moment to consider her options. "I guess that brings me back to young Andy." She eyed him sideways. "Though I'm not sure I like how alike the two of you are. In that *general* way," she added when he felt his face scowl. "You know, dark hair, blue eyes, square jaw. People might think the baby was yours."

The heat in his blood went from merely irritated to downright lethal.

"Okay, I won't go there. I'll just have to make sure young Andy is excited enough to tell everyone when he becomes a daddy. Do you know anything about his family?"

"Will you stop calling him young?" Josh rubbed his bleary eyes, willing away the idea she'd conjured of her and Young Andy Raymond. Damn, now she had *him* doing it.

"Who? You mean Young Andy? Young, young, young Andy Raymond." She was too damn giddy about ruffling his feathers.

"Youth isn't everything when it comes to sex. In fact, it's usually detrimental." He leaned toward her, remembering what his initial purpose had been coming out here. Her smile faltered and her hands stilled. "Experience goes a long way."

"That's a good point. Maybe not Andy. I mean, if I'm going to sleep around, I might as well enjoy it."

Oh, for the love of God. "You're not sleeping with anyone!"

"I don't remember asking permission, Josh." She rose to her feet, putting her hands on her bare hips in a few lithe movements he shouldn't have noticed. Unnerved at facing her waist level, he stood too. Unfortunately, for him, the space between the two lawn chairs they'd been sitting on didn't allow for two adults to stand. He ended up wrapping an arm around her still-wet form to steady them both, and she pressed flush against him. The mixed smell of coconut lotion and Miranda, tempered by chlorine and wide green eyes blinking in surprise, dizzied his senses.

Or maybe it was just feeling her again, his body automatically taking her weight as if it still remembered the one time he'd been allowed. The time he'd been trying for years to forget. Now it was impossible to ignore the electricity he'd only ever felt with her. The air around them crackled almost audibly. His arm tightened on her at about the same time that she rose on her tiptoes and tentatively pressed her lips to his.

She'd kissed him before, so long ago that he'd almost fooled himself into thinking it wasn't very memorable. It all came rushing back now, though. He deepened the kiss, running his tongue gingerly across her bottom lip, asking for entrance, which she willingly gave. His arms tightened on her waist, pulling her closer, making a tiny moan escape her. Her fingers wound their way into his hair, twirling his nerves like a yo-yo string. The kiss quickly escalated from gentle to a raging, breathless embrace.

Her breasts flattened against his chest, every inch of her

molding to him like warm clay. Someone groaned, deep and pleased. In his belly, the hunger he could usually tamp down practically rattled against its chains. His fingers slid over her slick skin, massaging and pulling her tighter. But it wasn't right. He shouldn't be devouring her this way.

Still, he couldn't stop. If her own hands, dancing through his hair, holding him just as close, were any kind of sign, she didn't want him to. Which wasn't exactly the point...How, after all these years of avoiding exactly this, was he failing to stop himself?

He wasn't a kid anymore. Mistakes like this couldn't be forgiven twice. As hard as he told himself to stop, his body was ignoring him and doing whatever it damn well pleased. His hands were roaming over her back, her ribs and threatening to go lower when another little groan sounded gently in the back of her throat. Suddenly all good sense vanished. He plundered the sweetness of her mouth, wallowing in the forbidden taste.

How many times had he wanted to kiss her again, just to see if it would be the same as it was when they were kids? Each time he'd sensed it coming, he'd said something stupid to upset her. This time, she didn't give him the chance. He pulled away from her lips, alternately kissing and nibbling down the left side of her neck, his fingers probing at the clip at the back of her bikini bra. Just as he felt the loosening of material, he heard a voice that yanked them both out of their sensual fog.

"Hey Josh, you here? Door's open." Raul Montenga.

Miranda stiffened in his arms. Her eyes met his. "Raul's here?"

He nodded. "He's moving back home. Joining the station." Taking Danny's place.

Her hands scrambled around her back for the straps. Josh shushed her, putting the hooks back together and letting go.

With his leg, he pushed the lawn chair back, making a god-awful scraping sound, but it gave him room to separate from her completely.

She smoothed her hands over her top, shaking. "I'm almost too grateful to think about how practiced you are with bra clips."

He made himself smile as Raul came out onto the deck.

"Hey! I've been bellowing. Why didn't you answer?" Raul was still wearing his dress blacks. His dark eyes narrowed on the two of them, flicking from one to the other before he smiled, wide and—unfortunately for Josh—as dirty-minded as ever. "Damn, girl, look at you."

Miranda blushed, moving slightly closer to Josh, he assumed for cover. It would serve her right if he let Raul get an eyeful, but against his better judgment, he turned, allowing her to find whatever refuge she could. Raul clearly didn't miss the gesture. He raised a brow, but said nothing as Josh spied her terry wrap. When he bent for it, her fingers curled into the back of his shirt.

He flipped the wrap over his shoulder. "Miranda was just leaving."

Behind him, she gasped. The hand at his back gripped tighter.

"Hot date, Randa?" Raul strolled off the deck toward them, unbuttoning the heavy black jacket.

"Something like that," she replied, tone brittle, nails sharp against Josh's spine.

He looked over his shoulder at her, stifling a growl. "Don't even think about it."

Cat green eyes crackled. "Just you try and stop me."

ଔ

"I gotta hand it to you, Josh." Raul dropped onto the deck chair Miranda had abandoned, having watched her storm out the side gate with enough interest to notch Josh's blood pressure up another ten points. He even picked up her beer and took a long pull. "I have never seen anyone piss her off quite like you. Or as often. Makes a body wonder why she keeps coming around."

"Yeah, well, you've been away from home a long time." Raul had moved up to Seattle ten years ago. He came home for visits often enough, but he wasn't as well in the loop as everyone else in town.

Raul's laugh did little to make him feel better. "I've lived two states away, not Mars. And your sister still talks to my sisters."

"Which one?" Raul had eight.

All Josh got was a shrug. "Pick one. They're all *cheppas*."

"Your sisters don't know everything. Miranda has a temper like a firecracker. Anything sets her off." Even simple things like common reason, justifiable cause, gravity...

Raul's eyebrows rose. "You can't possibly be that dumb."

"What?"

"In thirty years, you haven't noticed that the only one she has ever—and I mean *ever*—gotten mad at is you?"

Josh frowned. That wasn't possible. On the other hand, it would explain why she blew up on him like Mount St. Helen's all the damn time.

"And believe me, she has opportunities. You should see the way people treat her." Raul took another drink, then sighed as he let his big body relax fully into the chair. "But she never says anything. If my mother liked *gavachos*, she'd parade Miranda around my sisters and tell them to learn proper manners from the vestal virgin."

"What are you talking about? People love Miranda." From the time she was a little girl, she had the whole town eating out of her hand.

"Sure, that's why no one would sit next to her at the funeral except me."

Josh stared at the fence door, the latch firmly closed because Miranda had slammed it hard enough to splinter it.

"Danny's mother wouldn't even look at her when she gave her condolences, and you know Jennifer Randall is the nicest mom anyone ever had. She's looking for you, by the way. I told her you had the plague." Raul waited three whole beats for some response, then shrugged and continued. "Seriously, I've seen Mafia mistresses get better treatment at a funeral than she did. It's like every single person there blamed her for his death." Raul gave a shiver. "She never said a word to nobody though. Just took it in stride like she has every other shitty thing that happens to her. You got anything to eat? I'm starving."

Josh squinted an eye at him. "You just came back from the reception. There should have been plenty of food."

"No offense, but you white people got weird ideas on how to feed a crowd. I never saw so many cold cuts in my life. There was a lot of pie though. Damn lot of pie."

Josh snorted, despite himself. The funeral reception for Danny had been more like a Fourth of July picnic. His parents had wanted him celebrated like the hero he was, and since there were literally hundreds of people coming, it seemed best to give them a barbeque-style dinner. Raul had probably eaten enough to fill three horses.

"At least when *we* put out meat, you have a general idea

what part of the animal it came from. Last time I ate with your family, your Dad tried to feed me some poor animal's crispy fried ass."

Raul laughed, getting out of the chair as Josh led the way back into the house. "You don't know what you were missing, man. Just wait 'til he makes you some brain. *Madre de dio*, you'll die, it's so good."

"Yeah, that's what I'm afraid of." But his mind wasn't on the good-natured teasing. "When you were talking about Miranda, you don't mean people were actually mean to her, do you?"

Raul already stood at the open fridge, pulling out a fresh beer. If Josh didn't miss his guess, his old friend's shoulders stiffened briefly before he closed the door. The gauging expression on his brown face didn't leave much to the imagination, though. "What'd you think was gonna happen, man? You made it real clear she was no good for him. Even *I* heard about it."

"I *never* said she wasn't good enough for him." He knew he'd taken her dating Danny like an ass, but he would never say anything like that to anyone. If anything, Danny wasn't good enough for her, and Danny was the best man he'd ever known.

"Ch—yeah, guess everyone in town must have gotten their signals crossed because you've spent your whole life talking about what a walking disaster she is."

She was.

"And how she's never met a moment she couldn't get into trouble."

She hadn't.

"Or how if it weren't for you she'd probably have gotten herself killed or married to the first idiot to rub up on her."

Josh coughed, not liking to admit that he'd said those things in the past. Except the first idiot thing. Unfortunately, he knew exactly what had happened to that guy.

"Personally, I don't get why people listen to you. It's clear you don't see straight when it comes to Miranda. You never did." Raul walked past him out of the kitchen, hitting the swinging door a little hard. Josh followed, frowning. "But she's got the reputation as the town flake thanks to you. The girl who can barely tie her own shoes broke Danny Randall's heart. The women can't stand her and the men think she's poison. A leper'd have a better social life in this place."

Raul settled in the recliner and looked around for the TV remote. He found it without much effort and settled back as if that was all there were to say.

"Were they *mean* to her?" Josh reiterated, strangely having to hold onto his temper.

Raul didn't look up from the basketball game he found. "No one slapped her, if that's what you're after. But if it weren't for me and your sister, I don't think a single person would have said a word to her. And not a damn one of them felt bad about it either." He finally lifted his gaze, skewering Josh with a look that made him feel less than an inch tall. "Makes you wonder what Danny would have thought about that, doesn't it? I mean, she did break his heart. But he never held it against her. Or *you.*"

Josh wanted to ask why Danny would, but they both knew. He'd done everything he could to make them both feel like they'd cheated him of something. The unforgiving old flame who'd guilted Miranda until she broke the engagement. Raul had never judged him for his interference. In fact, no one had. Everyone seemed to agree that Miranda wasn't right for Danny, no matter what Danny said.

Josh had never once thought to consider why.

"Shit." He turned away, looking for his keys hanging on the peg by the door next to his coat. He'd have to apologize to her. Apologize for everyone in their small-minded little town. And he'd have to do it now, or his conscience would never let him sleep. Worse, he'd worry. The last time he'd left her alone to grieve a loved one— "I gotta go."

"Tell Miranda I said hi."

Josh considered saying something else to his friend, but the longer he took, the more likely he'd find the same kind of mess he'd found twelve years ago. A cold sweat broke out on his back and he rushed out the door.

Chapter Three

That damn man. Miranda stood in her shower, letting the hot water wash off the chlorine and hopefully her anger. She wasn't mad at Raul for interrupting. Or even at Josh. Much. She was mostly angry at herself for putting this ridiculous plan into motion. For attempting the impossible, especially on the day Danny should have been most important instead of just a reminder of how fleeting life could be. But she'd had a plan and Danny, God bless him, would have understood. He would have told her that she could think of him later.

Shame vied with pain until she sobbed into the spray. She had always thought of him later. That had been the crux of their problem together. She never had him on her mind or in her heart. And now, there was no more "later" for Danny Randall.

It didn't feel real, that someone so vital could be gone in a moment. He'd been so perfect, so much what every woman in her right mind was looking for. Those California golden-boy good looks, chocolate brown eyes and a sense of chivalry that was lost on most men today. He was always thinking of other people first, their wants and needs. More often than not, it was Miranda's wants and needs he was thinking of, even after their brief relationship ended.

Memories flowed sadly through her. Growing up with him

and Josh, as much his friend as she was Trisha's or Penelope's. Amusing him as much as she frustrated Josh. Being the center cog in their trio of friendship. But that all changed the first day he'd kissed her. She hadn't responded, but he promised to change her mind. The continuous flurry of his attention, slowly growing more and more beyond friendship. By the time she realized he was in love with her, so had Josh. She couldn't hurt Danny, and he was so sure she'd love him sooner or later. No matter how she tried, it just couldn't be done. When he proposed, she had accepted, though somehow she knew that it would never come about.

Her fighting with Josh had increased, peaking that day in Jimmy's Grocery when he saw the engagement ring...

Even now she couldn't remember what they'd been arguing about or who threw the first thing, just that Danny had walked out long before things had started flying. She knew he'd seen something then, and that night had brought their engagement to a short and sad end.

"I'm not angry, Miranda," Danny had said in the voice of a man who was too tired to keep fighting. "I was the stupid one to think I could ever matter more to you than him."

"Danny, please." She'd needed him to hold on, but he only shook his head.

"I'd do a lot of things for you, Miranda. But I won't settle for second-best. It's just not how I'm made." He silenced her with a look when she began to speak. "If you've ever cared about me at all, go. Before I hate us both for changing my mind."

She had gone, and to this day she wasn't sure if it was because he had asked her to or if she'd just seen her escape and taken it. It didn't matter. The result was the same—Danny got hurt and the blame for it would always fall on her. It would have been kinder never to get his hopes up. Never to have lifted her own.

Sitting crouched in her shower, Miranda cried at the thought of Danny being dead and his never having found the right person to love. He'd gone through a whole lifetime and found no one. And he'd had been so deserving of it.

Then there was Josh. Everyone could see Danny's death eating him up. He'd lost weight—she could see the hollows in his cheeks, the weariness in his shoulders and his walk. Did he even know how angry he was? She could feel it vibrating out of him every time he looked at her. He probably blamed her, same as everyone else.

It was almost enough to make her wonder if people might be right. The initial reports were that Danny had stepped right into a critically weakened portion of the roof. He should have seen the worn tears in the aluminum. Could he really have made such a critical mistake because he'd been preoccupied with her? Or by the fact that Josh was below, hating him *because* of her?

She could ask question after question—no answers would ever come.

She didn't know how long she stayed in there but the water was cold and her skin wrinkled when the sobs finally subsided. Aching, heartsore, she dried her body and slipped into the ratty red bathrobe she'd had since she was a kid. Hugging herself, she wandered out of her bathroom and screamed.

"Wh-what are you doing in here?" Breathless, she clutched her robe to her chest once she realized the man sitting on the foot of her bed was Josh.

He held up her spare key by way of explanation. She recognized it by the green key cover she'd put on it for him.

"I was worried about you," he said, looking miserable.

It didn't take much to figure out why. The night of her

parents' funeral was permanently burned into his memory.

Too tired to fight with him, she didn't bother being insulted. She simply nodded. "As you can see, I'm fine."

"You were fine that night, too."

Her spine tightened so fast she almost thought she heard it crack. She'd told him she was fine. Said it so many times she'd lost count, desperate to make him leave. That night, she hadn't wanted his pity. Hated how much she wanted him, needed him to want her back. But he hadn't. He'd been the same over-responsible Josh, treating her like another little sister. He'd have been the same with Trisha if they lost their mother. That night, she'd been young enough, wounded enough, to feel his pity like a blade instead of the support he'd meant it to be. If he hadn't come back...

"I'm not going to try to kill myself, Josh." Especially since the strongest thing she kept in her medicine cabinet these days was vitamin-B caplets.

He nodded, eyes cast downward, but she could see he didn't believe her. She hadn't succeeded in ending her life that day, but she'd most assuredly killed any kind of faith Josh Whittaker ever had in her. Odds were, he'd sit there at the foot of her bed until dawn, just to make sure she didn't find some way to harm herself. And he said *she* never learned...

She wiped her cheeks with her cuffs one last time and reached for her earlier confidence. It was shaky at best, but it would have to do.

"Shouldn't you be entertaining Raul?" She moved to sit at her vanity, stopping only to snitch the key out of his fingers and toss it on her nightstand before she grabbed her comb. The tremble in her hands was impossible to miss when he rose to stand behind her. The comb came down on her lap with a muted thump. She stared at Josh's reflection but the dim bedside lamp did little to illuminate the shadows on his face.

"He's only staying with me for a few days. He'll be fine on his own."

"Well, if you came to change my mind—"

"We both know you never had any intention of sleeping around, so why not just drop the pretense?" His voice sounded flat in her ears. Not angry. Not frustrated. As if he were stating an obvious fact. He was, really, but she could still hate that he felt he could dictate anything about her life.

"Because how I get pregnant isn't important. The fact is I want a child, Josh, and you're never going to allow it." She turned in her seat to face him. "What you're failing to understand is that I'm not asking your permission."

He crouched before her, showing none of the anger she expected. The blue of his eyes was dark, almost haunted. The shadows around his face could have been the dim light, but she didn't think so. And when he spoke, it was soft, as if she was fragile. "What really brought this on today? Penelope is probably telling you that medical options take time. You trust her a hell of a lot more than you do me, but you're still pushing me like a freight train headed uphill. Why are you so desperate?" His lips flattened into a hard line. "Is it because of Danny? Because you buried him today? Is that why you're pretending to want me?"

She knew the question cost him. Could see the bitterness it left on his face. Would he let her answer? Or believe her if he did? "Yes and no."

Surprisingly, he didn't interrupt.

After an expectant minute, she sighed. "Danny always wanted a family. A big one. He used to talk about wanting kids coming out of his ears."

Josh nodded. "I remember."

She shrugged, feeling the pain build in her again. "He never got them. He deserved them and he never had time for his dreams to come true. But I'm still here and I don't deserve what I want."

He shook his head. "Yes, you do. Don't talk like that."

"No, Josh, I don't. I've made so many mistakes. I hurt people. I hurt Danny."

"Miranda—"

"I hurt *you*," she whispered the crime that weighed the heaviest on her. "I ruined your friendship. You couldn't even go to his funeral because of me."

He reached up to cup her cheek in his palm, wiping her tears with his thumb. "I couldn't go because of me, Randa. Because there's a lot I didn't settle with Danny. It wasn't just you. You don't need that on your shoulders. I couldn't watch them put him in the ground. I couldn't. I especially couldn't sit around some damn picnic table, swapping stories about him with people waiting to see if I was convincing enough in my pain. No matter what the people of this town think. It was between me and Danny. Don't do it to yourself."

She closed her eyes and leaned into his touch. "But it *is* on my shoulders. It's always there. How many people I've failed. Everything I've screwed up. I have so much to give and now there's no one left who wants it. My parents are gone. Danny's gone. You." Even now she couldn't finish that sentence. "I thought, maybe, if I had a baby, I could finally have someone to love. Now that idea's dead too."

She had to turn her gaze away from him. He looked like she was ripping something out of him with every word.

More tears spilled over her lashes and she hugged her arms around herself, wishing he would just go and leave her alone. But he wouldn't. He wouldn't leave her alone tonight if she begged. Especially if she begged. “Just...don’t hate me tonight, Josh. I’ll get myself together, just please, don’t hate me right now.”

He took hold of her chin and made her look at him, his face catching the light and his eyes seeming to glow. “Hating you was never my problem.”

He tugged her toward him and, boneless, she went. His arms tightened around her, warm and full of the strength she’d been longing for. She sagged against the wall of his chest, her forehead to his pulse, her fingers resting over the steady beat of his heart. The shudders faded gradually, seeping out of her. Wanting him closer, she twisted and lifted her arm to slide over his shoulder, clasping him to her.

Her eyes closed when she felt his mouth nuzzle into the terry of her shoulder. His hands spread across her back, wide and supportive. Was he holding her for her pain or his own? She pulled back, smoothing her hands on either side of his face so she could look down and see for herself. Josh locked so much inside, things he should forget, he should forgive, crowded in there without relief or release. Her hands retraced the harsh contours of his face, but all she could see were the shadows of pain in his eyes.

He wouldn’t tell her tonight about his hurt. His grief. He probably would never voice it at all. But she couldn’t take more hurt. Not his, not her own. Closing her eyes, she pressed a kiss to his cheek, wishing she could do more for him. If he could just let her in, share with her, he wouldn’t have to hold it all inside. But that was Josh. So she pressed another kiss to his jaw, wanting to soothe and take some of it away. Another touched the corner of his lips and she tasted the tears she’d spilled onto his face. He said nothing, but his hands on her back tightened.

She thought he meant to hold her closer, maybe even tuck

her head back to his shoulder, but instead, his mouth met hers, warm and soft. Gentle. Strangely, she didn't start in surprise. Just continued the small kisses over his lips, felt them being returned. Soon, they grew longer. Warmer.

Different.

She sighed into him, her whole body relieved to be in his arms, and his tongue caressed the seam of her lips. She opened for him as naturally as breathing, moaning at his taste when he stroked her own. Even with her robe in the way, his heat began to fill her. The ache of her regrets faded into a different ache. A hunger. A need, to comfort, to soothe. Her fingers wended into his hair, pulling his kiss deeper. Soon, their lips hardly parted at all.

Yes, this was right. This was where she belonged. This, she could do for him. For herself. He couldn't say the words or lance the pain, but she could. She opened her mouth more for him, whimpered at the urgency building inside her. His kiss grew hungrier. Demanding. So she gave. Her heart, her soul, she offered into that one unending kiss.

He tugged her against him, hands tangling in her hair as he turned her head in a way that fit his mouth more comfortably, devouring her. She returned the favor, every nerve ending coming alive like water in the sun. Vivid. Colorful. Sparkling. But she needed more.

Her roaming hands pulled his shirt from where it had been tucked. Unbuttoning the shirt was out of the question—buttons went flying instead. Josh's only response was a low chuckle she felt more than heard. His mouth left hers as he trailed kisses down the column of her throat. He found a sensitive spot, just below her ear, nibbling until her nails started to dig into his skin.

"Please, Josh." The words tore from her as she tugged his

open shirt over his shoulders. She wasn't even sure what she was asking for. One more moment? One more night? Forgiveness? Or for the love she knew she was equally unlikely to get? It didn't matter. Tonight, she needed him to be there and he was. She needed to give what had been trapped inside her, locked away inside him. She had to. Even if she didn't have the courage to ask why.

He stopped kissing, stopped everything, to look in her eyes. But she didn't want to know what he was looking for. Tired of guilt, tired of being afraid of what he'd find if he would just allow himself to see, she closed her lids and kissed him again. "*Please.*"

For precious seconds he remained still. Silent. For a heartbeat, she thought he might leave her, that he'd peel her off his lap and tell her how close they'd come to a mistake. It was nearly enough to make her cry... Until he did the unexpected and lifted her into his arms.

When she felt the softness of her bed at her back, she finally released the breath she hadn't meant to hold in. She never quite got it back again. Josh lay down next to her, untying her sash to find the still-damp skin beneath. Soon, she was bare on the bed beneath him, shuddering a breath when their skin met, trembling where his fingers touched. He tested her flesh with his hands while she tried desperately to hold in the whimpers he seemed determined to draw out. Then he began tasting...

He nibbled her ribs, one at a time, grasping her hips in each hand and lifting her so he could wreak havoc on her vulnerable belly. Her breasts grew warm and swollen under his ministrations, becoming so sensitive that all he had to do was breathe on them to make her quiver. All the while, she smoothed her palms over his shoulders and the muscles of his flanks, learning the hard contours and shapes of the man, so different from the lean lines and sharp angles of his youth. She couldn't touch or taste enough of him. Her senses were starved for him and it was a special kind of torture to know she'd never have her fill.

He lay above her, gently rocking her with his every motion. He slipped his arms under her shoulders, cradling her against him and entangling his hands once more in her hair. He kissed her chin, her cheeks, each eye, her nose and with a satisfied smile, lowered his lips to hers to take her over completely.

He made love to her with his kiss, and if the rest of her wasn't still tingling, she'd have even forgotten she had a body. He was still rocking them, only now he used one hand to mold her side to him, cupping her bottom before steering her thigh to open further and wrap around him. He followed suit with the other, so fluidly she hadn't been aware until she felt herself pressed intimately against him.

Then, suddenly, every one of her molecules were completely aware of him and only him. Nothing else in the universe could possibly exist other than this moment and the heated expression in his eyes. God help her, but she'd been waiting to see it her whole life. And she had very little hope of ever seeing it again.

Once will have to be enough, she thought, as she felt her body welcoming him home to her. He murmured into the hollow of her throat, words she could barely understand. Inside, her heart broke a little, the curl of hope extinguished before she had a chance to know it was there.

"Just this once," he murmured again.

She clutched him tighter, pushing the whispers out of her mind. If she had her way, she'd never let him go. But she couldn't hold him forever. The moment would come when he'd leave. And she'd have to pretend it wasn't killing her. At least when he was gone, she'd have this moment for the rest of her life. She mourned losing him even as she felt and followed the rhythm he set. She arched into his deep strokes, felt the tension in her body coil tighter and tighter. She cried out only when she looked into eyes that had been passion-stained to a deep cobalt and knew she would never be satisfied with anyone or anything else.

ঔ

By morning, Miranda had disappeared.

She lay there next to him, warm, soft and tempting, but something in her eyes, the way her entire body curled away from him in the tangle of sheets, told him she was gone in all the ways that mattered. She had a way of locking part of herself away, hiding her emotions behind a mask, and simply going away from reality. Away from *him.*

He hated that mask.

The harder he tried to get past it, the more she buried herself. From other people, he could understand, but when she used it against him it burned like the worst betrayal. She let him kiss her goodbye, a too-serene smile on her lips. She even nodded when he said they'd talk later, but when he came back with some of those giant croissants she liked, her windows were shut; her doors were locked; even her stupid dog was inside. Bad time to have forgotten to reclaim the key.

He called, reaching only her answering machine. At first, he'd hang up, but as days, then weeks, passed, he left messages. He asked her to call him back. Or come by. Or even to call his mother, just so he'd know she was okay.

Apparently, she wasn't.

He knew better than to pound on her door—the town

gossips would set up shop on her bedraggled lawn—but he couldn't stop himself from driving by, hoping for a glimpse of even her shadow. Any sign that he hadn't just screwed up the most important relationship he had left.

No sign came.

He should never have slept with her. Bad things always happened when he gave into that temptation. As if that lesson hadn't been drummed into his head a long time ago. He and Miranda made lousy lovers—if one didn't count the sex—but her friendship, even her enmity... He didn't know what he'd do without them. If he could just get her to talk to him, he could fix things. They'd go back to the safe friendship they'd maintained for decades. No more touching. No more bikinis or talk of promiscuity. He'd even try to deal with his anger at Danny if he had to, but there was no telling her until she surfaced. Until she came to him.

The irony was, he had no idea what the hell to say should that small miracle happen. Miranda could derail the best-plotted plans with just a blink of her cinnamon lashes. He wasn't even totally sure how they'd ended up in bed together. Almost two months later and he still didn't have an excuse he could use. Just a consuming want that grew hungrier and more desperate the longer she hid herself away. So he buried it under his anger at how easily she cut him out of her life.

How the hell do you just do that to a person? He hadn't understood it as a kid and he sure as hell didn't understand it now. She knew how crazy it would make him. Which meant she was doing it on purpose just to drive him insane.

But why?

Which is usually when his mental diatribes became circular.

His mother even called him to report that Miranda hadn't

been in contact and what had he done? He'd said precious little in his defense, but then again, he had no intention of discussing his sex life with his mother. Trisha landed on his front porch with the same question because Miranda hadn't returned any calls or responded to threats yelled up from her front porch. No one else seemed to care that she'd all but vanished from their small town. Which only made him angrier.

Things at work weren't any better. Since fire season was in full swing, they had more staff to trip over, not to mention training of the volunteer search-and-rescue teams to deal with. And somehow, it seemed every one of them was aware not only that something had happened with Miranda, they also knew that she wasn't speaking to him. But at least on the latter, they could always tell when that was happening. It happened too often, although usually for much shorter durations. The last time it had gone this long was when Miranda and Danny were engaged. Even that milestone had now been surpassed.

Everyone either stayed out of his way or just did what he said, including Raul, who was technically now in command. All Raul did was shake his head and mutter something unpleasant in Spanish. Young Andy, as Josh had begun thinking of him, seemed to have acquired invisibility. Apparently, he'd been particularly hard on the little guy. Josh had a rough time feeling bad about that one.

To put it kindly, Miranda's silent treatment had thrown his life into an epic shithole.

So he was understandably surprised when she simply sauntered into the firehouse while he was playing cards with Raul after dinner, sending every man there into open-mouthed shock. She'd dressed up, her makeup set to deadly, the crisp white outfit hugging curves he could taste, just looking at her. Everyone else just wished they could.

Despite the palpable lust tingeing the air, he didn't like the way she looked. Dark circles still bruised the skin under her eyes, her hair lay a little limp around her face and he could see the weariness in her step. She walked stiffly and her jaw could have been wired shut, but damn if she wasn't the best thing he'd seen in a long time.

She also seemed to get a whiff of Willie Wilde's infamous Atomic Chili. She slowly turned green before a word came out of her mouth. Dropping her purse, she quickly turned to her right and ran toward the bathroom.

"Miranda?" He retrieved her purse and followed her. The sound of retching made him want to join her, but instead he grabbed a towel from the rack by the door and hurried to her side. He held her head for the interminable moments of her violent vomiting. Out of breath, she leaned against him without argument, sprawled over his lap, shuddering in careful breaths. How the two of them managed to fit on the floor of that stall, he couldn't say, but if she hadn't been throwing up, he almost would have called the moment nice.

Probably because it was quiet.

He wiped her mouth with the towel and flushed the toilet for her. "Better?"

She nodded miserably. "I throw up if I smell water, much less what passes for food in this place." She'd lost weight, he could tell by the feel of her. Exactly how long had she been sick? He wanted to ask, but it didn't seem the smartest question to start with. Maybe something she'd consider more sensitive, like, where the hell have you been?

"I'm pregnant," she suddenly blurted out, dropping her head into her hands and sobbing.

He'd been about to say something, but for the life of him, he couldn't remember what it was. Neither could he explain the warmth spreading through him, making him want to smile at her. Or the sheer terror that made him want to clutch the toilet like she'd been doing.

What the hell was he supposed to say?

Clearly, she expected something. Doleful green eyes peered at him, waiting for judgment. For the first time in years, he didn't have any to offer. He couldn't feel a thing beyond the shock. But he'd better. All that came to mind was the truth.

"Isn't that what you wanted?" he asked softly, barely finding his voice. He reached out a hand, brushing it against her cheek. She fought for a second, her lids fluttering closed before she turned her face into his palm, the way she always had. But this time, the moisture from her eyes burned into his palm.

"No, not like this." Still lying on him like an old dish rag, her voice sounded mournful. Did she regret shutting him out? Or did she only regret sleeping with him? "I didn't plan things like *this*. I wanted you to want this baby, too. I wanted it to be celebrated. I *wanted* us to be happy. To do this like calm, rational adults."

He almost laughed. "Why? Neither one of us *is* a calm, rational adult."

She stayed quiet for a few long seconds. Long enough for Josh to start to worry. Silence and Miranda were better off mutually exclusive. "This is new, you admitting that."

"Well, I don't want to ruin this little announcement of yours by arguing."

"Where's Josh Whittaker and what have you done with him?"

Relief flooded him at the sign of spirit. "Are you okay to get up or do you need more time?"

She shook her head and he helped her to her feet. Watching her carefully, he escorted her to the eight-foot long basin that was the communal sink. Above it hung a mirror of equal length. Miranda sniffed at her reflection.

"Whatever happened to glowing? I look like I got run over by the fire truck." She elbowed him in the ribs when he nodded.

"Hey, I never said I'd lie to you." She set up a toothbrush she pulled from her purse along with a travel-size tube of toothpaste. At least she was prepared, which made him wonder just how many times a day this happened. "You don't look like you've been taking care of yourself. Or my baby," he added, frowning at the strange proprietary feeling in his chest.

Her eyes widened. Then narrowed as she pierced him with a sharp green glare.

"*Your* baby?" she replied around the toothbrush. She was ridiculously cute with a mouthful of suds.

"Like it's anyone else's."

"Actually—" She spit into the sink. "I came to talk to Raul. If you'll remember correctly, I'm not speaking to you."

"Fine job you're doing there, sweetheart. Turn up your nose a little more, I can still see the freckles." He crossed his arms.

She rinsed out her mouth and made a show of repairing her lipstick. "For your information, I don't have freckles."

He snorted at that. "Yes, you do." He gazed at her up and down, remembering each dip and curve of her. Every smooth inch and unique flavor of her skin. "Everywhere."

She dropped her lipstick into the sink. After a second, she pushed out a breath. "No reason to get rude, Josh."

He smiled as she reached down to pick it up, but it felt more like a show of teeth. Did she think he was going to let her play her games with a child? *His* child? "No reason to get mean, either. Both of us know that baby is mine."

Did she sense something territorial in his tone? She must have, because she finally got some color in her cheeks. Crap. So much for not arguing.

"No, this baby is mine. *Only* mine."

"Excuse me?" He couldn't believe she'd just said that as if it was supposed to make sense.

"*I* wanted a baby, Josh. Not you. Why would you claim it?"

"Because it's mine." If she thought he was going to allow his child to be speculated on by an entire town, she needed serious therapy.

She rolled her eyes. "It's always black or white with you, isn't it? Right or wrong, yes or no, yours or mine." She turned to face him, yanking a paper towel from the dispenser. "Are you saying that you want to be part of this baby's life? That you want her to call you Daddy? That you're going to change diapers? Take care of her when she's sick? Be there for her when she needs a ride to school?"

"What's this 'she' stuff?" His brows drew together in consternation. How could she be thinking of school? The kid hadn't even finished dividing cells yet.

"Are you going to tell your mother?"

He felt the blood drain out of his face.

Her mouth pursed. "I didn't think so."

"That's not fair, you're not afraid of my mother." And she should be. Billie Phillips was not going to be thrilled about her grandchild being conceived out of wedlock.

"If *you're* afraid of your mother, this baby is too much for you already."

"Miranda," he groaned as she shoved away from the sink. "I know what goes into a baby and yes, I have every intention of being part of his life."

She caught the "his", but wisely said nothing about it.

"You'll have to deal with me on a fairly regular basis, Josh. Like an adult."

Josh struggled to keep the grin off his face. Using his own argument against him? At least she hadn't lost her nerve with her stomach contents. "I have to deal with you all the time, anyway." He shrugged. Besides, treating her like an adult wouldn't exactly be a hardship, now would it? It wasn't like they could brush this pregnancy under a rug the way he'd planned to ignore their night together. That was a crappy plan anyway. All it took was watching her walk into the room and that gnawing need to touch her damn near ate him alive. He wouldn't have lasted five minutes if she'd crooked her finger his way. Maybe now he didn't have to fight it. They could go a different route, one that left no question in anyone's mind whose baby she carried. Particularly Miranda's.

Her eyes widened, as if she could read his mind, and she backed up a step. "There'll be no more of..." She struggled for a delicate word, cheeks pinking nicely. "...the other."

It took him a full thirty seconds to get what she was blushing about. He raised his eyebrow. "The other?"

Oh, she was going to squirm over this one. Maybe if she hadn't locked him out. Maybe if she'd been responsible and told him their night together was too much for her, he could have walked away. Could have tamed the wanting. Might have been able to let her go. But he'd lost the ability to ignore how much he wanted her the second she crossed the firehouse threshold. For two solid months, he'd done nothing but think about her and wonder what he'd done wrong. Ached for her. Did she really think she could just shut that off at will?

If she did, she realized her mistake now because her eyes

registered all kinds of feminine panic. He advanced on her slowly.

She started backing away. “You know what I mean, Josh.”

“I do?” He noticed she was slowly getting closer to that wall behind her. Yep, there it was and she’d just pinned herself against it.

“Josh,” she warned, but by now he was only an inch or so away with a hand on each side of her. So close he could take a deep breath and touch her all along his length.

“Yes,” he replied, but he knew it was a command, not a response.

“Josh, please.” She put a hand to his chest, but forgot to push.

“Okay.” He smiled just before dipping his lips to hers. Her eyes fluttered closed as he leaned into her and a whimper escaped her. Just then, the door opened and they both turned their heads to see who it was. If Young Andy didn’t immediately wish he were anywhere else, he didn’t have the sense God gave a gnat.

“I’ll just go and…I’ll just go.” The kid actually turned red at interrupting what was obviously an intimate moment in the men’s room.

Miranda took the moment to escape, ducking under his arm and sprinting for the door. “We can talk later,” she called after herself, leaving Josh with the boy.

Unfortunately for Josh, the kid’s gulp of fear wasn’t nearly as satisfying as what he’d just missed.

☙❧

No one is expecting a fire tonight. Cool early summer

evening. Crickets singing. Somewhere in the hills, a few coyotes are howling. It's like a fucking movie set or something. My teeth grind just listening to it.

Something is going to burn tonight though. An old cabin no one uses anymore, on the big hill above the lake. I heard it used to be a make-out spot for kids, but before that, it was a trail spot. And a favorite hiking stop of Josh Whittaker's. I knew about it well enough, in old stories that got told over and over again. Josh and his dad, spending time together like out of some fucking black and white TV show. But now it's just an old cabin. A pile of sticks.

Kindling.

Burning things is always a rush. Watching them explode is even better. I light the match and flick it into the shack. Nothing happens at first. I wonder if maybe the match went out in the air, but then a little glow starts to flicker in the broken windows. My glow. Like something magical is going on.

Something magical is.

The fire bursts, a fat flower of sparks and light, spitting and spinning to life. The building takes on the orange light, becoming a giant lantern, putting off heat I can feel yards away.

I watch the fire tear through the roof, listening to the wood crackle and groan. I know I have to get further back once it starts to lick at the propane tanks, but it's hard to tear my eyes away. *He* should be feeling this pain, not the building. The helplessness of burning and not being able to do anything to save himself. But he will. Soon. Soon.

Finally, my legs start backing up without my permission. I turn my head and start to run. I can feel the growing tension as the flames look for something else to eat. They can smell the propane waiting. Like me, they're hungry. Angry. Enraged.

I'm going full speed through the hard dirt now, sending up

a cloud with every step, skidding as much as I am running. Almost all the way down the hill before the inevitable boom hits.

I'm laughing even as I hit the ground. I only get up when I hear the sirens screaming up the hill. In the dark, they'll never know I was here.

Chapter Four

Trisha Arbourdale's ten-month-old sat peacefully on her lap, a pacifier in her cherubic mouth. Trisha's three-year-old twins were happily tearing Miranda's backyard apart with the help of an exuberant Rusty. Giggles and barks lit up the neighborhood. Unfortunately, they had little effect on their mother's expression.

Her friend, who looked so much like Josh, her blue eyes wide and her mouth still in the shape of an *O*, nearly dropped her hard-earned daughter.

"E-excuse me?" she stuttered.

"Josh and I are having a baby." Miranda repeated, slowing her voice almost to phonetics.

Trisha managed to put her mouth back together. "You're putting me on." She laughed. She kept laughing despite Miranda's serious expression. "You can't be serious."

Silence.

"Oh my God, you *are* serious. How did this happen?"

Miranda winced, her face burning while she wished Trisha had some sense of decorum. Any at all. Instead, her friend had a smug, slightly dirty smile on her face.

"The old-fashioned way." The chuckle was definitely dirty. "Well, well, well. No wonder you haven't been answering my phone calls. You never could keep a secret. How long have you two been at it?"

"Trisha!" Though Miranda should have known better than to be surprised. Trisha was a blunt, up-front kind of woman and absolutely nothing shocked her. At least, not for long. "We haven't been *at it.*"

Trisha looked doubtful.

"We haven't. It was only one night. I haven't been talking to anyone."

"One *night*?" Leave it to Trisha to seize on the least important part. "Not once? Not twice? A whole night?"

Miranda decided to quit trying to talk. Trisha got along fine communicating with the flush crawling up her face in waves.

"Hell, I have all kinds of new respect for old Joshie-pooh." Trisha picked up the baby's hand to fan her face. The baby giggled, making even Miranda smile. Charlotte had the typical Whittaker coloring. Her mother's dollopy black curls, pink chubby cheeks and a little bow mouth. Would her baby look like this? Or would it be like herself, a red-haired trouble magnet?

"You gonna tell me how this happened or not?"

Not. Honesty would get her nowhere but deeper when it came to Trisha. "I am not discussing your brother's sex life with you."

"We're discussing *your* sex life, it just so happens that Josh is part of it. Besides, you haven't had a sex life since, sheesh, I don't even remember, and I remember everyone's sex life. Come on, tell me details and I'll just pretend it's not my brother. Please, Miranda, soaps don't do it for me anymore," Trisha pleaded, laughing when Charlotte mimicked the sounds.

"What about Michael? Doesn't he give you your daily

infusion of romance?"

Trisha looked skeptical. "Michael and I have been married almost eleven years. I love him dearly, but romance is not a daily occurrence these days. And with three small kids, it's damn hard to achieve at all. We get by and when the kids get older, we'll get back to our gratuitous sex life. Provided, of course, that Michael gets that vasectomy I demanded."

"You don't want any more children?" Miranda would have a whole houseful of kids if she could. That was one thing she and Danny had agreed on. Neither of them much enjoyed being an only child. Friends were great, but there was something lonely about going home and having no one to laugh or talk with.

"No." Trisha's laughter subsided abruptly. "I love my kids. But if I have another one, not only will I probably blow up into a whale, the odds aren't good anyone will come out of the pregnancy alive. Trust me, three is enough for us. We're even happy when we have enough time to stop and think about it. So, tell me about you and Josh."

"There's not a lot to tell. He was worried about me after the funeral." She shrugged. Trisha didn't know about the incident with her mother's pain medication. She wasn't bringing it up to explain why Josh thought she was so fragile he'd be willing to have pity sex with her. "One thing led to another."

"Uh-huh."

Miranda blinked at her friend. "What?"

"You really expect me to believe *my* brother, *Mr. Judge, Jury & Executioner*, just magically gets over his raging jealousy and comes over to your house to forgive you for almost marrying his best friend?"

"I—I wouldn't call it jealousy, exactly."

"That's because you're an idiot. When it comes to Josh, you're dumber than a turkey in a rainstorm."

Miranda clamped her mouth shut in surprise.

"He's jealous and angry and if he had an honest bone in his body, he'd admit it's all completely his fault. But he doesn't, so he won't and that's how I know he didn't just accidentally stroll over after the funeral to offer comfort and support in your mourning. Because Josh doesn't forgive anyone. Anything. Ever."

This, Miranda knew.

"Which means you *did* something to make him come over."

"I did not!" *Specifically.*

Trisha's shrewd glare almost made Miranda squirm in her seat. Almost. "Honey, no one—and I mean no one—can work my brother in a circle the way you do. Not even my mother and that's saying something. And one of the biggest reasons you're among my nearest and dearest is that you're a guiltless schemer. Plus, I just like to watch you torture him. So just cough up what you're up to. I'm not gonna be mad."

"I didn't plan this!" *Exactly.*

"Did you know you only blush on the left side when you're lying?"

Now that was just stupid. Still, Miranda brought her hand to her left cheek.

Trisha leaned forward, looking her over as if she was going to find some kind of evidence on her face. "You don't even know what you've gotten yourself into, do you?"

Under that too-knowing stare, fear rippled in Miranda's belly. But Trisha didn't have the whole truth and she wasn't about to get it out of Miranda. "What I don't know is what kind of drugs you've been taking. You're completely insane." But there wasn't enough confidence in her voice and she could tell Trisha knew it.

"He's going to figure it out, Rand."

Miranda's stomach plummeted but she didn't allow herself to flinch. Let Trisha think she chose Danny. Sure it meant her friend thought she was a pathetic woman out to trap her man with the oldest trick in the book. Trisha would think less of her than maybe anyone else in town, but Miranda could live with that. Her true relationship with Danny was the only failure she could keep to herself.

"I don't know what you're talking about."

"If I don't miss my guess, you got pregnant on purpose. If he wasn't a moron, he'd know already." Trisha reached out a hand to grasp the one Miranda was clenching the hem of her blouse with. "I know you probably thought that was a good enough reason to do this, but it's not going to change his mind, honey. Baby or no baby, Josh isn't going to forget you chose Danny over him."

Miranda stared blankly. Mute. There was no explaining the truth. No way to come out of it with any dignity. Josh might be angry about her relationship with Danny, but that wasn't the crime he couldn't forgive. If she wanted her friend to understand, she'd have to tell Trisha about her suicide attempt. Then Trisha would have her pick of shames to hold over Miranda's head for the rest of her life—trying to kill herself or spending the last twelve years longing for a man who'd never forgive her for it.

"Why do you do this to yourself?"

"Do what?"

"Turn yourself inside out for him!" Trisha's sigh lacked any sisterly devotion. "I know he's my brother and God knows, I love him. That doesn't make me blind to his faults. He's difficult, exacting and so stubborn he makes a body want to punch him sometimes. But he's family and he's good to me. You? You I don't get. Sometimes I think all he ever does is hurt you. Anyone else would send you to an abuse clinic for therapy. Or maybe just a CAT scan."

"What are you asking me, Trisha?" And could she get to it quicker, because Miranda suddenly felt worn out.

"I'm asking why you love him. What miraculous thing could he have done to make you so loyal to a dream that's never going to come true?"

Miranda considered not answering, but Trisha's earnestness promised a lack of judgment. She really just wanted to understand. "Do you remember the day your father left? For good?"

Trisha blinked, a small frown forming, then a nod.

"He wasn't supposed to be there that night, that's why my parents let me stay over. Some sort of trip for his job, but he got fired instead. He came home and started yelling at Billie." The fighting had lasted all night. Miranda and Trish had huddled in Trisha's bed, small hands cupped over each other's ears, terrified.

"Josh came into our room, remember? He didn't say anything. Just brought his blanket and his pillow and lay down in front of the door."

Trisha nodded. "He always did that when they fought. My father would have killed him if he'd come in angry and tripped over him. But it made me feel safer, so Josh did it."

Miranda nodded. "And later, when Jared's bags were packed and he was finally leaving, we all sat on the porch and watched him go. Me, you, Billie. Except Josh. He stood by the front door like a sentinel, making sure every last thing of Jared's was out of the house.

"You were crying and your mom was holding you. But no one held Josh. So I went over and I held his hand. He never looked at me, never said anything, just held my hand so tight my fingers hurt. Even after Jared drove away and you and your mom went inside. For a long time it was just me and Josh, watching to make sure he didn't come back. He eventually let go, but by then my entire life had changed."

Trisha looked at her silently for a long time. But this was Trish. Silence never lasted long. "I still don't get it. What's so miraculous about sleeping on the floor and holding your hand?"

Miranda laughed, sagging back in her patio chair. Sometimes her friend really didn't know how good she had it in the family department. "Even when he was a little boy, Josh was a protector. A hero. He knew exactly what your father would have done to him if he'd gotten in the way of Jared's temper. He was six years old, probably just as scared or maybe more than we were, but he did it anyway. Because that's who he is. He'd give up his life for anyone in this town, for anyone in trouble. It's not a death wish, he just truly believes someone has to and he's willing to do it. How do you *not* love a man like that?"

Trisha gave a sheepish grin. "All right, I'll give you that. My brother is the bravest man on the planet. But what's the handholding got to do with it?"

Miranda shrugged. "It was the moment I realized no one else knew he needed protecting too."

"And that's kept you going for twenty-seven years?" Trisha's disbelief made Miranda laugh.

"No. Believe me, it hasn't. It's not like I sat here at home, wasting away, waiting for Josh every day of my life." Even if that's what it felt like sometimes. "I had pseudo-crushes in school. Guys I dated here and there." Until Josh made his presence known and whatever almost interesting guy she was with disappeared, practically in a puff of smoke. She opted not to mention that. "But I always came back around to Josh."

Trish snorted. "Because he doesn't give you any choice."

"No." Though that was true. "Because he's still the guy who would lay down in front of the door to protect me from whatever might be on the other side. And," she added when Trisha attempted to interrupt. "Because I still know I'm the only one he can let down his guard with. So, yes, your brother is stubborn and hard to deal with and can drive me absolutely crazy when he sets his mind to it, but that doesn't change the basic truth."

"Which is?"

"I love him." Didn't get any more basic than that. "And under all the mistakes we've made, disasters that have happened and the mess we've made of it, he loves me. I have to believe someday we can make it work."

"My parents loved each other too," Trisha reminded her sadly. "Love isn't a guarantee. Sometimes, it just gets to kick the shit out of you."

Miranda dimmed. It wasn't a guarantee. And so far, the boot marks on her heart had been pretty rough. But she couldn't stop her heart from wanting. From hoping. "I had to try, Trish."

Her friend took her hand and squeezed it supportively. That was the best thing about Trisha. She didn't always understand, but she remained unwavering anyway. "I just hope to God this doesn't blow up in your face."

All right, mostly unwavering. "Thanks. I feel so much better now."

Trisha sighed. "I'm only trying to keep you from getting your hopes up. And I can tell I'm probably too late to say this." Her gaze flickered to Miranda's belly. "Waaaaaaaaaaay too late."

Miranda rolled her eyes.

"But I don't want you to get too hurt. You've always expected so much from him. I finally get why, but that's a high pedestal you keep him on. If you don't want him to fall, don't start thinking that by having his baby you're going to have Josh, too. It won't happen."

Miranda opened her mouth to argue, but Trisha shushed her.

"It *won't* happen. Maybe it's because of the way my dad was. The way things had to be after he left. I don't know, but something broke in my brother a long time ago and nothing you or anyone else does is gonna fix it. He doesn't understand how to let things go."

That wasn't true. If there was one thing Josh knew how to do, it was let her go.

"I didn't plan this," she heard herself saying again to Trisha's pitying expression.

"I don't know if that's better or worse."

Neither did Miranda.

Trisha called her kids to her and gave Miranda a brief hug. "I am happy for you, honey. I know you've always wanted children. Once you're broken in, you're going to be a great mother."

"What do you mean, *broken in*?" Miranda asked as the kids gathered their things, grumbling.

"Oh, you know, getting used to no sleep, sharing all your food, no sense of privacy or personal space. Hair pulling. Kids are really big on that one." Trisha gave her a bright smile. "Honest to God, Rand. I can't think of any luckier kid on earth. You're gonna love that baby 'til it screams for mercy."

"Why doesn't that sound like a compliment?"

Trisha hitched a shoulder, gesturing to the boys to follow her to the side gate. Disappointed to be leaving, they kissed the dog, and then Miranda, goodbye.

☙❧

Josh never did get his hands on young Andy. He had to hand it to the kid, he was fast. So Josh spent the next few hours wrapping his brain around the idea of a baby. Somewhere deep inside Miranda's tiny body was a tinier baby. A little miracle for her, a bloody nightmare for him.

His hands hadn't stopped shaking since she left. A baby. A child that would look to him for comfort, support, God help him, for safety. Probably from its mother. At least he could teach that lesson: there *was* no safety from Miranda. She was like a hurricane, permanently parked in his life, throwing every defense and piece of stability he could build in every direction.

But really, what did he know about taking care of small children? Babies were loud, so easily breakable. He could make the wrong move thousands of times, a prospect of sheer horror. On the other hand, his father had managed not to kill him or Trisha when they were babies, which meant infants had some kind of impressive resiliency. How soon would he have to set the right example? Worse, he'd have to trust others to take care of the kid while he worked. The worries could drive him to a coronary before the kid even came out.

Part of him wanted to shake Miranda for putting him in this damnable position. Another part of him wanted to pick her up and swing her around in exhilaration at the impossible gift she was giving him. A child. Their child. A glimpse at would could have been if he'd made the right choices years ago. All because of a wrong choice made now.

Rationally, he knew he couldn't really blame Miranda for their situation, but oh, how he wanted to. He could've used protection, could have stopped himself from making love to her at all, but he'd somehow managed not to think of either. Not making love to her that night would have taken a miracle. As for the protection...well, there was no excuse. Even if it hadn't occurred to her, usually his brain could be relied on to think for them both. Something about her tears, though, always managed to short-circuit his ability to see the right path to take. All he could ever do when she cried was try to make it better.

Well, he could consider that a job well done.

When the fire alarms went off, it was almost a relief.

He cut off his personal life and was able to concentrate on stopping the brush fire along the Broken Horse hiking trail. It hadn't gotten far, just up one side of the hill and down into the wooded valley where the lake overflowed in the winter. He knew the trail like the back of his hand, having spent so much of his early childhood summers being dragged from one end of the trail to the other while his father worked the property. Damn shame to see it charred and dead. But eventually, the fire was out and the cleanup complete. In the end, he was right back where he started.

Confused.

As soon as he was off-duty, there was only one thing he could do. He drove to Miranda's, wanting answers he couldn't be sure she had. He found her sleeping across the swing on her porch. After all these weeks, it seemed strange for it to be so easy to find her. Now that he had her, what the hell was he going to say?

Taking a moment to revel in the peace on her face, he watched her swing back and forth in the late afternoon breeze.

Her soft skirt caught the wind, rippling over her ankles while she hugged a pillow to her face on the opposite arm rest. Red curls spilled this way and that, twisting an urge into him to slide them off her face. But he knew better. They'd fall back the way they wanted. Miranda did everything her own way.

How she'd managed to survive this long in life sometimes amazed him. She couldn't balance her checkbook without an accountant and a bloodhound. She found trouble, usually the life-threatening type, on a monthly basis. The woman was asleep on her own front porch, for Pete's sake. If he checked, he'd no doubt find an unlocked front door because she had no sense of self-preservation whatsoever. She was a shameless pack rat and her dog was a brainless hundred-pound ball of fur that had yet to figure out he wasn't a lapdog or a world-class breeding stud. Between the two of them, they were madness and mayhem unleashed.

But she could also make a person laugh in the worst moments of their lives. She could calm children when their whole lives had burned down nearly on top of them. He'd seen her do it after wildfires had taken half the town. She'd been arrested twice for breaking and entering when a friend of hers needed help escaping an abusive mate, and she never failed to stand up to the gossips if she thought they were wrong. No matter how reckless she was or insane she might drive him, she would always be the fun-loving girl who'd jumped off the roof of his garage when she was eight just to impress him.

And he'd always be the guy who wished he could catch her.

But he hadn't deserved her as a kid. He sure as hell didn't deserve her now.

She murmured something in her sleep, her nose wrinkling at the same time. When she slept, he'd swear she was five again. It was the only time she truly looked innocent. Her brow knitted and she mumbled again, but he couldn't quite make out the words.

He kneeled in front of her. "What's the matter, Rand?"

"Don't wanna be alone."

"You're not, honey." He gave into his urging and brushed her hair off her cheek.

She sobbed, hugging the pillow tighter. Tears slid soundlessly from her clenched lids, tearing at his heart.

"I'm right here, Miranda. Don't cry. You're not alone." He lowered his forehead to hers, cupping her cheek in his palm. She jolted, her lashes lifting. So close, her eyes were deep jade. Sleepy. Enthralling. Unable to stop himself, he leaned in to kiss her slightly parted lips.

She warmed to him immediately, wrapping her arm around his shoulder. The kiss naturally took on more heat than he had intended, but God help him, he could not pull himself away from her. Her hands entwined in his hair, pulling him closer. She seemed to be lazily drinking him in, as if she had all the time in the world to twist him around her little finger.

Only Miranda could drug him with a kiss. Her soft lips drew all his reason and logic out like poison from his soul, leaving him wrecked and senseless, unable to do anything but come back for another taste of her. Just as he had back when they were kids. And the night that they'd made the baby nestled somewhere deep inside her.

It was fair to say he was intoxicated when he hefted her into his arms and carried her into her house. All the way up to her bedroom. Miranda came silkily to life, kissing his face, his jaw, his throat, running those hands of hers through his hair. In fact, he could hardly be held responsible for slowly removing her clothes while she wordlessly removed his.

Their coming together was inevitable, he realized. Like a

need for air. He needed to touch her, taste her again. Simply be with her so he could feel like himself again instead of the confused, angry person he'd become when she locked herself away. Driven by his insatiable thirst for her, Josh pushed her to the edge over and over and over again until she cried out his name in absolute surrender. Then and only then was he able to let himself go.

Afterward, cuddled together under her blankets, he had no idea where to begin. Worse, he wasn't sure he wanted to.

☙❧

"Josh?" Miranda still wasn't sure what happened. One second she was lying on the swing, thinking of the fruitlessness of her feelings, and the next, Josh was there, filling the hollow ache inside her, touching her face, kissing her and giving her all the affection she craved. Would she be an idiot if she asked why?

"Hmm?" He kept his face pressed to her chest, cradled in the circle of her arms. He ran a hand over her, tracing the bare curve of her hip to her waist and back again.

"What are we doing?"

She felt him smile against her skin. "If you don't know, I can show you again."

A smile tugged at her own lips. "You know what I mean. I can't keep falling into bed with you this way..." She trailed off, not wanting to sound as if she was asking for more.

He shifted backward, reaching for a scrap of her hair, playing absently with it. "I don't know what this is. But it sure beats fighting." He turned the strands to brush them across the sensitive skin of her breast.

She curled her fingers around his to hold him still. “That is not conducive to a serious discussion.”

He kept his gaze on the bare flesh in front of him, letting go of her hair so he could tease a soft nipple into a hardened point. “No, they aren’t.”

She swatted at his ever-busy hands. “Really, Josh. What are we doing here? I mean, are we just playing? When this burns itself out, what are we going to do then?”

She didn’t kid herself. Josh never stayed with a woman for long. And her own pathetic charms never held him. Rational thought dictated he was happy to have sex with her because the horse had already left the barn. Pregnant is as pregnant does, it seemed.

His sigh could have moved mountains, but he kept her limbs tangled with his when she made to move away. “I’ve never been the kind of man who does anything without a plan, you know that.”

She nodded. She held her breath, terrified what kind of plan she might find herself agreeing to. Would she find herself some kind of weekend girl, available whenever he asked? God, that would kill any feeling she ever had for him, for once and for all.

“But right now, all I know is that I can’t go back to the way things were, and I’m sure as hell not going back to being kicked out of your life.”

She waited, but he seemed out of words. “I’m not hearing a plan, Josh.”

“Don’t got one, Rand.” He tugged her closer, tracing her collarbone with his lips.

Against her will, her eyes closed. Warmth began to pool in her belly. But... She took hold of the hair on the back of his head and pulled. “Josh!”

Deep blue eyes showed only sensual disapproval. “I don’t know if you noticed, but I’m kinda busy down here.”

“I want to know why you keep sleeping with me.”

And he didn’t want to give her the answer. Or, she realized when his mouth softened and his eyes lost their seductive gleam, maybe he really was as confused as she was. Because all she could see was how much he needed her, needed her to not push him away again. Instantly, whatever barriers she had left against him melted away.

Turkey in a rainstorm. Again.

“Can’t we just...see what happens from here?”

She wanted to say yes. It was the chance she’d waited her whole life for, it seemed. But it was also a chance to give him absolutely everything she had left. And get nothing back.

If it were just her, she knew she was impulsive enough to say yes and not regret a thing. But she had more then herself to think about now.

“What if you hate me when it’s over? What about the baby?”

A frown clouded his expression. “No matter what happens between us, I’m going to be a father to my kid.” Yes, she could see that. He wouldn’t leave his child behind the way his own father had. It didn’t take a genius to see Josh had built his life around being everything Jared Whittaker wasn’t—loyal, protective, *kind.* He forever questioned his own worth, but Miranda didn’t. Their baby would never question her father’s dedication to her. And through him, she’d always have Josh’s family. She would never be alone.

Heart pounding, she gave him a shaky smile. “Okay. We’ll see where it goes.”

She felt his relief in every suddenly relaxed muscle of his

body against hers. "You know it's impossible for me to hate you, don't you?"

No, but it was a nice moment and she didn't want to ruin it, so she kept her smile.

He touched her lips with his, a caress that whispered with promise. "Miranda."

Change of subject needed. "Did you happen to call your mother yet?"

If she didn't know better, she'd think he growled.

"Because I've already told Trisha. It's only a matter of time before the news reaches Billie in Florida."

"And everyone else in all the states in between." His grumble was halfhearted at best. He'd started nibbling on her neck, most likely to derail her. She'd argue a few more seconds, just so he'd think not bothering to call was all his idea... "It's still early over there."

"Where?" Warm, calloused fingers found the curve of her hip while his kiss turned hot and wet over the cord of her neck. She arched into him, her eyes fluttering closed under the teasing assault.

"Um...Florida?"

"No, it's not."

She was pretty sure it was, but one of his hands slid over her backside and took hold of her so possessively she gasped. "My phone is on the nightstand. You can call her right now."

"No, I can't," he said softly, moving over her, pressing his hard length to the soft folds that ached for him to press deeper.

"Why not?" she asked, breathless with sensation as he sank inside, a satisfied smile on his handsome face.

"'Cause I'm busy." Then he kissed her and both of them forgot he even had a mother.

⁂

The bastard.

I've been watching all day, waiting for some sign of misery. Something to show this unfeeling prick ever cared about the shack. For a second there, I thought maybe. The way he stared at the charred roots of trees and the black rocks... But he just turned around and pretended nothing happened. The same way he did when they dragged Danny's body out of the warehouse.

Asshole.

I should have known someone like him had no sense of sentimentality. I'm burning the wrong things.

I followed him from the firehouse here to Miranda McTiernan's house. I watched him kiss her and pick her up and take her inside. I know what they're doing in there. Anyone on this block probably knows. Not that they'll give a shit. They all expect it anyway.

The sun falls behind the tree line and lights come on everywhere but Miranda's house. I could probably break in right now and they wouldn't notice. I could walk right into that room and do to him what he did to me. Take away the woman who matters. Who loves him.

In my head, the memory is clear. The yelling voices, her shriek when he'd shaken her, angry because he'd seen the bags by the door. She'd started to cry. To plead. But he was too drunk to hear her. Angry because of Josh. Drunk because of Josh. And when he'd shoved her, yelling at her to get out, he hadn't cared where he threw her. Not until the cracking sound of bone on the stone hearth made it past the booze.

Will Josh just stand there while I crush Miranda's skull? Will he stare while the blood floods out of her head into the flames and her eyes stop seeing anything at all?

Probably not.

He needs to break more before I take her away. He needs to be stripped of everything he knows and loves, every sense of security, before I take what means the most. I could move faster. Burn it all in a blinding rush, but I'm not ready for this to end. I need to savor it. Make it worth all the years I've had to wait.

Eventually, he'll put the pieces together. Who I am. Why I'm doing this. He'll know everything I'm taking from him. And he'll ask himself if there was anything he could have done. Any way he could have saved them.

Like me, he'll never know for sure.

Chapter Five

Miranda stared at her sock-encased wriggling toes while Josh studied a magazine extolling the values of a good prenatal diet. He eyed her suspiciously and she knew he was trying to guess her weight.

"Don't even try it, Buster." As if he possibly could, what with the shapeless paper gown the nurse had her don.

He smiled. "This is supposed to be a *good* doctor's visit. Not to mention she's your friend. What could she possibly do to you to make you *this* nervous?"

"You wouldn't ask if *you* ever had to be in stirrups."

Before he could respond, Dr. Penelope Gibson came in with a smile and a folder, reading it as she entered. "When you asked about fertility charts, I had no idea you'd make such quick work—*Josh!*" She quickly covered her surprise as Josh stood to shake her hand. She gave another quick yelp when her nurse bumped into her from behind. Darting her dark blue eyes around Josh, Penelope quirked her mouth in silent question.

Miranda smiled weakly. It's not like she wouldn't have to get used to the confusion. Penelope's surprise would be mirrored all around town and a hell of a lot less tactfully.

Penelope had her dark hair pulled back into a French braid, tied neatly with a red bow. Her smile reached her deep blue eyes, while her heart-shaped face turned up to greet him.

Penelope could best be described as the third musketeer to Miranda and Trisha. As tactful as Trisha was tactless. The women still went out once a month to keep up, and Penelope was more than aware of Josh's usual relationship with Miranda. Miranda braced herself for a phone call later, one bound to be full of questions far more probing than Trisha's could ever be.

"So, let's get a look-see at the new little guy." Penelope prepped her machine almost by rote, asking questions about morning sickness or any discomfort.

Miranda answered, but her toes curled tighter inside her socks despite Penelope's gentle distractions. Penelope indicated for Josh to stand on Miranda's left side, as the ultrasound machine lay on her right. Then Josh noticed the instrument in her hand. Miranda could tell because Penelope had gestured with the long, wand-shaped apparatus and Josh's frown followed the swishing motion. Penelope hummed to herself as she squirted lubrication on its tip.

"Where exactly do you plan on putting that?" he stepped forward in an attempt to take it from her. Miranda quickly grabbed his hand and pulled him back.

"It's an internal ultrasound," Penelope explained with a small grin. "At this stage of the pregnancy, it's the only way to clearly see the baby."

Josh eyed the wand warily.

"It won't hurt her, I promise. Believe it or not, I've had experience with this kind of thing." She smiled, but Josh didn't look all that assured. Come to think of it, Miranda didn't feel reassured either. The few times she'd needed that thing hadn't been particularly thrilling. But she couldn't have Josh protecting her from Penelope, of all people.

"It's fine, Josh," she whispered.

His clasp on her hand loosened. His eyes narrowed as she put her knees up under the sheet and lay back while Penelope discreetly inserted the cool device. Miranda flinched at the intrusion, squeezing her fingers into knots. She caught Penelope's calming smile and forced her muscles to relax with a slowly releasing breath. She laid her head back on the crinkling paper and watched where Penelope directed.

Suddenly, an image burst onto the little screen. Both she and Josh sucked in breaths. Little white blobs blinked in front of them. At first, it looked like a continuous tube of light while Penelope shifted the wand, and then the blur clarified into two little lima bean shapes pulsing bright and brighter.

Miranda's eyes stung and filled as she watched for movement. She'd waited her entire life to see something so incredible. She couldn't tear her eyes away even if she wanted to. Not even when Josh's grip on her hand bordered on painful. They stared, silently, as Penelope magnified the view.

Josh turned his head to the side, skewing his angle to match the little bean shapes. "Are those feet?"

Penelope chuckled, but didn't reply. Instead she turned to her nurse. "Helen, maybe you should find Mr. Whittaker a chair." Attention back on the console, she pushed a few more buttons and the screen split into two—a still image and the moving one. Miranda heard a small printer whirring and a curling paper rolled out near the base.

"See this bright spot near the top of the bean?" Penelope tapped a finger to the screen. "That's a heartbeat."

Miranda's heart stopped.

"But there's two of those spots," Josh replied, not sounding upset or concerned. And he should be. She knew him. If he put together what she thought she'd just put together... He *would* be.

The nurse nudged the chair by the wall toward the exam table.

Josh spared her a brief glance before returning his gaze back to the screen. “Why are there two?”

Penelope’s upper lip twitched. “Because the other baby would have some serious problems getting by without one.”

“Other baby?”

And now Miranda knew what a wax version of Josh would look like. She had to give him credit, though. He didn’t crumple into the chair. But he eyed it. Longingly.

Penelope must have mistaken that for acceptance because the friend in her escaped her doctor demeanor and she squeezed Miranda’s hand and laughed. “Congratulations, guys! It’s twins!”

But all Miranda heard was the thump of Josh’s towering body hitting the ground.

ઉ

While they drove home, Josh behind the wheel, silence reigned. Not a particularly comforting silence.

Josh replayed every aspect of the examination after the humiliation of his knees buckling. How Penelope assured him not every set of twins were as “energetic” as his sister’s, but that occasionally, these kinds of things did seem to run in families. How she had claimed that all looked secure and safe and he didn’t have to worry. However, if Miranda wanted things to continue in such a vein, she would have to be careful because multiple pregnancies were much higher risk and far more taxing to her body. That part scared him.

He remembered some of the rules from Trisha’s pregnancy,

but he made Penelope outline them for Miranda, just in case. No strenuous lifting of any kind. Running wasn't out of the question, but she'd have to brace herself for a vast reduction because she probably wouldn't be able to run much past the third month. Maintaining walks might be a good solution since strong legs would aid in the birth, but again, only as long as she was comfortable. Since Miranda had quite a bit of trouble sticking to a healthy diet of any kind, Penelope admonished Josh to make sure that Miranda cut her junk food by half before the end of the first trimester. Miranda smarted at that, but kept quiet. In fact, he glanced sideways at the pensive expression still on her face, she'd been quiet ever since. Just the way she'd been the night they'd conceived.

Josh re-gripped the steering wheel, his suddenly slick hands having lost their hold. If Miranda was quiet, she was thinking. And Miranda's thinking generally got him into trouble, physical pain, or debt. Since Penelope had informed him that pregnant woman had magnified emotions and responses, he naturally began to fear for his life.

At the very least, life as he needed it.

"You're not going to disappear on me again, are you?"

When she didn't answer, he darted a glance away from traffic. She kept her face to the window.

"Miranda?"

"What?" Flat tone. Almost complete lack of interest.

Damn it. "You're locking me out again."

She peered over her shoulder at him, her eyes brimming with tears. She turned back when one splashed down, startling her. Biting off a swear word she'd usually hit him for using, Josh swerved to the side of the road and parked the car in front of Ben Friedly's place. The ancient old guy was probably across the street at Shaky Jake's anyway.

"You can't do this, Miranda. Not this time."

"Do what?"

He reached over the stick shift to cup her cheek and pull her face back to facing him so he could look her in the eye. She could ignore many things, but she'd never once been able to reject the way only he could touch her. She didn't this time either, which made the sting of her tears scald his hand until it shook.

"You disappear. The second you find yourself on any kind of limb, your eyes go glassy and you go so far inside yourself that I can't see you anymore."

She batted at his fingers but he didn't let go. Finally, she yanked herself free. "I'm not disappearing, you ass, I'm angry. I'm allowed to be angry, aren't I?"

His brows rose even as he surged with relief. "Angry? At what?"

He didn't feel so relieved when she glared. "At you, you idiot."

"Me? What did I do?" He'd asked questions. He'd taken part. He didn't break that damn stick thing Penelope used. He'd been a frickin' saint in that office.

"You *fainted*, Josh!"

He had to swallow a growl. "I didn't faint. My knees gave."

She snorted her opinion of that. "Since when do *your* knees give? You carry people out of burning buildings over uneven terrain all the time. But take one look at two embryos and you practically wet your pants!"

"I did not!" At that point, all feeling below the waist had gone regrettably numb but even he hadn't gone that far.

"You did too!" Tears streamed unchecked while she swung out to his shoulder. "What's so terrifying about two innocent, sweet, tiny, incredibly fragile, emotionally vulnerable little people?"

Josh's temper dissipated as she sobbed openly into her own hands. He reached out to touch her heaving shoulders, not sure what would happen if he did. At the last second he pulled back. "Miranda? What's really wrong?"

Her hands came down, her whole body jolting with hiccups while she dragged in air. "What's wrong? What's *wrong*? Are you stupid? There's *two people* in me!"

"Um—"

"How the hell am I going to get them out, Josh? Did you think about that? *Did you?*"

He gaped at her. Definitely not answering that question.

"Oh my God, two! How am I going to...do...*anything*?"

"Miranda." He reached for her but she batted his hands away.

"No! I thought I could handle one baby alone. I can do that. But two? By myself?" If she wasn't careful, she'd hyperventilate.

"You won't be by yourself."

"Oh yeah?" Even through tears, the sarcasm couldn't be missed. "Who's gonna be with me? You? With your fabulous trick knees? The first time they cry you'll probably fall out of bed and knock yourself unconscious."

"Miranda." Okay, *this* he could handle. She wasn't mad, she was panicking. And who could blame her? She just got a hell of a lot more than she'd planned on. Anyone would freak out. She just needed reassurance. A calm voice. Steady hands. He took hold of hers, bringing them together across the console. "You're not going to have to do this alone. I promise. At worst, we can always hire some extra help."

Uh-oh. Not a single quiver to her breathing now. Her lips

took a mutinous twist and she wrenched her hands away. "You can't promise this away, Josh. Especially not by promising to *hire* someone to be a parent for you."

"That's not what I—"

"Just stop, okay? Stop trying to make me feel better." She didn't start crying again, thank God, but this resigned misery was almost worse. Especially since she kept shifting away from his touch. Suddenly, he had to reassure her. To make her feel safe with him, even if terror danced a Russian troika down his spine.

"I'll be there. I have always been there for you. I always will be. You aren't going to raise these kids alone."

Dewy green eyes met his, calm and heartbreaking. "You didn't even want one baby, Josh. And you've never wanted *me*. Now you're stuck with us and it's only a matter of time before you start to resent us for it. What other definition for alone could there be?"

He wanted to answer her. Wished he were capable of giving her the words she needed. But they wouldn't fit through the vise of his throat. Finally, she turned away, back to the glass. Silence never accused so loudly.

He started the truck and eased back into traffic.

Hours later, Josh still couldn't shake the guilt he felt about leaving Miranda after the appointment. He'd tried to extend his time with her, not wanting to leave her alone. Not wanting to go with her still looking at him like...like that. He couldn't put a name on what emotion glimmered in her eyes. Not anger, not sadness. Just something that made his chest ache and made him want to hold her until it was gone. But there was no getting close to her, not today. He left making sure she knew he'd be back and he'd expect her to be there when he did.

When her look turned defiant again, he knew she'd

understood.

Still, Miranda floated in his mind like a specter, those green eyes haunting him while he stepped through the firehouse door. Those eyes and the memory of two tiny blinking lights that shouldn't have brought a lump to his throat, but had anyway.

Everywhere he looked somehow reminded him of her. Her photos hung literally all over the firehouse. Over the years, she'd become something of a house mascot. She had gone with either him or Danny to all their functions and the evidence was abundant. Miranda, smiling in the black backless sequined number she'd worn to the Firemen's Ball, glittered at him from the long wall near the trucks. The three of them together at Danny's reception the night he made Captain. She and the other wives and girlfriends posing in their husbands' baseball uniforms. It had always been a source of secret pride that she'd worn his jersey, not Danny's, even if that picture was taken years before their trio had finally fractured. Others of the picnics, baseball games and parties drew him up the stairs.

One picture in particular he remembered putting up himself. Miranda, covered with mud, jumping on his back after a lost round of tug-of-war. Her dirty red hair spilled out from under his hat. She'd stolen it right off of his head, just to spite him for winning. Raul had taken the picture and Josh had always liked it, because they were both smiling. It always brought a new one to his lips. He usually told himself that it was only because it reminded him that it had taken a month to get all the dirt out of that thing. Not today, however.

Today, his mouth tightened into a grim line, because everything was different. Nothing would ever be the same again, either.

Josh threw his duffel bag on the ground and viciously kicked it under his bunk. Why did she have to look at him that way? As if she had every reason to doubt him. *She* was the flaky one. *She* was the one who couldn't get through a week without some kind of ridiculous emergency she needed him to save her from. *Josh, my kitchen faucet just exploded, there's water everywhere... Josh, Rusty got caught with Mr. Vivaldi's show dog again... Josh, something fell out of my car engine and I have no idea what it is...* She couldn't get through three days without him.

She did just fine without you for two months, his conscience reminded him.

And look how well that turned out. Pregnant with twins and sick as a dog.

He sat on the bunk and sighed, his shoulders sagging while he stared at the floor between his boots. The truth was Miranda had every right to look at him with doubt. Honestly, he was only surprised it had taken her this long. When it mattered most, he'd failed her every time. The fact that she'd survived was the only comfort he had. Doubting he could take on fatherhood, that he could keep two fragile beings safe and secure... He couldn't blame her for that. No one could.

But it still stung.

Leaving the bag and his frustration behind, he walked out to watch the guys scrub the truck. Though at least four guys worked on her, Josh found himself staring at Young Andy Raymond. He'd barely noticed the guy before Miranda brought him up. Ever since, he'd found himself looking at him and wondering what it was she saw in him. There was as much a passing resemblance between them as there was with any other guy on the street with dark hair and blue eyes. Other than his obvious crush on her, something had caught her attention about Andy, and Josh could not, for the life of him, figure out what it might be. But the more he looked, the more agitated he became and the worse their working relationship became. Not good for a guy who usually made it his business to train the rookies.

Unfortunately, Andy noticed he'd caught Josh's attention. He threw a glare at Josh before moving off the tail section of the truck to get to the front. Josh could almost blame the boy for this predicament with Miranda, but not quite. Even he knew the kid had nothing to do with his own stupidity. Still, he watched the young man and wondered at Andy Raymond's continued hostility. It wasn't like he hadn't gone out of his way to be nicer the past couple of days. He'd even apologized for taking his frustration out on him, and Andy had just stoically nodded and walked away. Clearly, it hadn't been handled.

Josh went to stand next to where Andy crouched, scrubbing the front left tire. Andy didn't acknowledge his arrival.

"You don't like me much, do you, Raymond?" he began conversationally, gazing out at the mountainous skyline.

"Not particularly, sir," Andy replied between what had to be gritting teeth.

"Any particular reason why?"

"None apart from the obvious, sir."

It didn't miss Josh's attention that Andy was scrubbing just a little too long and a bit too hard. "Take it easy on that wheel, boy."

Andy stopped, gripping the sponge tightly for a moment before throwing it into the large bucket next to him. He stood to his full height, an inch or two shorter than Josh, but still tall enough to make a decent threat. "Is there something you wanted, sir?"

Josh looked the younger man in the eyes; dark, angry eyes. Pride rippled up and down the younger man's frame. He was holding onto protocol with both hands, even if they weren't particularly martial at the Fifteenth. Definitely needed handling. "Just get it off your chest, kid."

Andy's eyes narrowed. After what looked like a hell of an internal struggle, he relaxed slightly. "No sir, I don't like you. I don't appreciate the way you've singled me out whenever you can't get laid. *Sir.*"

Josh heard the chuckles and general pointless woo-hooing of the other guys blatantly listening in. At least the kid had balls. Stupid, but he had balls.

Andy wanted to say a lot more, Josh could easily tell. Trisha had a look similar to that when she was holding back—not a common occurrence. Like steam rising without an outlet. And with the audience around them, the kid might just get brave enough to keep going. But martial or not, there were still rules to follow and the kid would learn them or he'd leave. Period.

"You're right. I did single you out. I shouldn't have." Josh turned a glacial gaze on the kid. "But we already discussed that. If you have a problem with me, you either get over it or transfer out. I won't allow anyone's, *anyone's*," he repeated pointedly for the entire crew, "life to be at stake because of hurt feelings. You bring your petty shit into a fire and someone could die, understand?"

Andy glared at him, his jaw tensing and releasing.

"I apologized and I was sincere. It's over. Move on."

The kid's gaze flickered from Josh to the people around them. After a second or so, he nodded his chin incrementally.

It wasn't much, but it'd have to do. Josh walked away feeling no better, disbelieving he'd actually bothered to pick at the kid without provocation. Still, he reminded himself, they *were* things that needed to be said. If Andy lost his concentration during a blaze, who knew what could happen? Josh didn't want to find out, and he didn't want anyone else to either.

Nevertheless, guilt doubled on him. He grabbed a clipboard off the wall and set off to do some inventories.

"You sure you're done tormenting the kiddies?" Raul's amused voice followed Josh into the supply closet.

"Not a good time, Raul." The boxes of paper towel rolls needed counting.

"Yeah, I can see how you'd feel that way, what with Miranda pregnant and all."

A box fell at Josh's feet.

"Did she tell you who did the deed?"

Josh stared at the box. White cardboard. Blue lettering. Same as usual. But how'd it get on the ground? And why did he want to stomp it flat?

Raul clapped a hand on his shoulder. The camaraderie failed to soothe. "Hey, you're taking it a lot better than people expected, if all you're doing is taking a strip off Raymond's pink fuzzy ass. Punk has it coming anyway."

"Penelope told you?" Josh turned, dazed. Wasn't there something illegal about discussing your patient's particulars?

"Penelope *Gibson*?" Raul squinted at him. Raul's smile took on a tinge of nostalgia. Penelope's crush on Raul back in high school was the stuff of legends. Unfortunately for Penelope, an embarrassing legend. "I haven't seen her once since I moved back. Why, is she looking for me?"

"Probably as much as she's looking for a horse to kick her in the face." She might even welcome the horse's kick first.

If Josh didn't know better, he'd think that was hurt on his old friend's face. "Hey, I never had any problems with Penelope.

She was my friend. *Sort of.*"

If one could call a quiet girl following you around school for five years a friend. Raul certainly hadn't back then, but Josh wasn't about to open that can of worms. "How'd you find out about Miranda?"

Raul's smile came right back to the here and now. "From you. You really ought to know better than to have a fight in front of Shaky Jake's, man. I heard one of the guys saw you two arguing and he snuck up next to your truck. The windows were closed but he managed to hear her screaming about two people inside her. I gotta tell you, from what I heard, they spent a good twenty minutes batting around possibilities for that. Those old guys in there are into some kinky shit."

"Raul."

"Anyway, May Belle finally figured Miranda was probably pregnant with twins." People generally listened when Shaky Jake's owner, May Belle Butner, said something was fact, as it saved a lot of time figuring out the truth for themselves, Josh reasoned while Raul continued. "Said screaming is kinda common when that happens. What no one can figure out is if they should be celebrating or feeling sad that Danny's never going to know his kids."

Josh wasn't quite sure what happened exactly. One second Raul was looking thoughtful and the next, he was blinking in surprise because Josh had his forearm shoved under the other man's chin, both their bodies slammed against the door.

"You wanna let go before I beat the living shit out of you?" Raul asked, voice strained but calm, bringing Josh back to reality.

Where he'd just attacked his commanding officer and good friend.

He let go as fast as he'd leapt. Raul cleared his throat,

waiting, but Josh didn't have the first clue what to say. Hell, he didn't even know what the hell he was doing. "Sorry."

Raul's brows rose. "That's it? You try to take my head off for nothing and that's all you got?" When he didn't elaborate, Raul crossed his arms. "What am I missing?"

Josh bent to pick up the now dented box. It wouldn't look right in the front so he moved a few to stuff it to the back.

Raul kept waiting.

Without any more boxes to adjust and the ability to count completely out of his head, Josh sighed. "Danny's not the father."

Raul blinked. Twice. Then his eyes widened like an eight-year-old. "Oh."

Yeah. Oh.

"You getting married then?"

"What? No!" God, no. He could still see Miranda's mossy eyes, wet and afraid. Marriage to him was the last thing she needed.

"So you're just going to let her go through this alone?"

"Why does everyone keep saying that?" Especially Raul, of all people. He'd left a string of women pining after him, including Penelope, without so much as a thought on how they'd manage without him.

"Maybe because you're not saying you're going to marry her." Raul tsked.

Did Raul think Josh wouldn't give everything he had for the chance to spend his life with Miranda? It wasn't an option. First, she wouldn't accept him, and second, he didn't have the right to expect her to. She deserved better.

Raul didn't seem to see his reasoning. "Then maybe it's for the best if people keep thinking the kids are Danny's."

Red stained Josh's vision.

"People are a hell of a lot kinder to a widows than they are to—"

"Finish that sentence and I'll rip out your goddamn throat."

Raul laughed, but the sound rang brittle in Josh's ears. "You'd better get used to hearing it, *cabrón.* It's what everyone else in this uptight little cow town is gonna say unless she gets married pretty damn quick."

Great, now Raul was going into macho overdrive. "She's not marrying me." Hell, after listening to her in the truck, he couldn't think of a way to convince her to.

"Well, you sure as hell fixed it so she's not marrying anyone else." Shaking his head, the other man sighed, kicking at a piece of nothing on the ground. "At least, not for a while."

"What's that supposed to mean?" Josh forced his mind back on track. He picked up his clipboard and looked around for his pen.

"It means you finally found a way to warn off every single guy for a hundred thousand miles. For as long as she's bearing your unholy spawn, anyway. Maybe a year or two after that. But then it's over, *compadre.* No matter what you do, how much you bitch, a woman like Miranda won't go to waste. Some lucky guy is going to see past the screaming babies and she'll be gone."

Josh shook his head, rejection still moving him when nothing else would.

"Oh yes, she will. Some other guys is going to find her and take care of her. Treat her like you're *supposed* to treat the woman you love. Then *your* sorry ass is just gonna have to get over it."

"Miranda wouldn't—" He cut himself short. Wouldn't what?

Do that to him? Wouldn't marry someone who loved her and cared for her? Josh's own mother had loved his father, to everyone's detriment. She'd had kids too. And when Nathan Phillips came along, she'd found real happiness, leaving Jared Whittaker to bury his bitterness in the bottle where he buried everything else in his pathetic life. Josh and Trisha ended up better because of it, too. A serious lurch in his stomach nearly made him vomit. After everything he'd done to avoid being like his father, he could well end up exactly like him.

"Of course she would," Raul went on, blithely. "She's not gonna give a shit what you think by then."

Of that much, Josh was certain. "No matter what, I'll always be the father of her children." Was that what Jared told himself, too? Were they both destined to be wrong?

"Yeah, but how many women stay in love with the asshole who knocks them up and leaves them to raise his kids alone?"

"I'm not leaving her alone!" He would be there. For all of them. He wasn't going to be like Jared, not in any way. He'd find a way to make her believe in him again. There had to be one.

Raul didn't flinch at the menace roaring in his direction. "All I'm saying, man, is this pregnancy is your last chance. You gotta figure out what it is you want. Either be a man and step up..."

"Or what?" he asked, knowing he wasn't going to like what he heard.

Raul didn't disappoint. "Or step out of the way."

Chapter Six

"*Keep her eating healthy, Josh...*" Miranda mimicked as she climbed out of her car. She slammed the door and hefted her purse onto her shoulder. Her own friend, one she'd had since grade school, and Penelope had still told *Josh* to make sure she ate correctly. Didn't anyone think she could take care of herself?

Didn't they realize she was the only one who would?

She stumbled in her indignation, dipping perilously close to a sob. But she'd wallowed in self-pity for a solid hour after Josh left her at her house. In the end she was still stuck with her situation and worse, she was hungry. That never led to good things. Rather than order a pizza to throw up later, she'd decided to go shopping. Handle her *own* health. Take care of her *own* baby. Er...babies.

She stopped, hand on her stomach, willing it to stop swimming around. A deep breath later, she walked toward the double glass doors of Jimmy's Market. Rancho del Cielo wasn't big enough to lure the larger grocery chains, which worked just fine for the town, but the prospect of going in was never more daunting than now. Everyone she knew shopped in the market. And since the fight in the store, it seemed all of them had an opinion about her. Either she was at fault for coming between two best friends or she was the biggest flake in three states, dumb enough to impersonate a fence post. Shopping these days usually required fast feet and all her reserves in patience. She wasn't confident in either at the moment. But if she wanted to eat, she had to go in.

The first thing to hit her was the blast of cool air from the air conditioners, soothing her like balm. The second was the gasp of interrupted conversation.

Great. If the flushed cheeks and plate-sized eyes of the teenager frozen in the course of ringing up a bag of chips meant anything, they'd been talking about her. The customer at the front of the line was Abigail McGee. Seventy-six if she was a day, the spinster had an opinion on anyone who did anything questionable.

She and Miranda were well acquainted.

"Miranda." The old bat nodded in her direction, guilt-free as ever.

"Miss McGee." It really sucked to so dislike your own kindergarten teacher.

Turning away, Miranda headed for the fruit section. Apples might be nice. No, watermelon. Cold, sweet watermelon...

Opting for the full melons, she headed for the deep bins full of the huge fruit. She'd always liked the colors of watermelons. Rich and green, striped, then vibrant red inside. She'd have to include it in her next Hannah the Squirrel book. As it stood now, she'd have to work double time to make her deadline, but her editor understood about the morning sickness slowing her down. If the watermelon was inspiring to look at, who knew, it might be even more inspiring while she ate. She dipped her head to knock for a ripe one, but instead of hearing the deep hollow thump of a sweet melon, she heard a whispered voice from the other side of the bin.

"Do you think she's *really* pregnant?"

Shock jolted through her. Was *that* what Miss McGee was talking about?

"Nah, she's always been an attention hound," another voice answered. "She's probably faking it for pity."

She was about to dry heave all over someone's Fourth of July treat. Standing up straight, she looked around and saw no less than four other people around the bins. Any of them could have been whispering.

Miranda backed away. Apples. She'd go with apples.

But it wasn't any better on that side of the produce department. Eyes she could feel watched her inspect the Golden Delicious until they felt like fire on her neck. She stuffed three in a bag and moved on to look for crackers. Penelope had mentioned crackers and ginger might help with the nausea. She'd just gotten hold of a box when Lola Velasquez strolled up with her cart. The older woman danced absently in place while she studied two boxes of crackers by waving them back and forth in front of her face.

"Miranda, *niña*, which one should I get?"

Startled, Miranda stared at the burgundy-coiffed hairstylist briefly before taking a look at the two boxes. One was white cheddar flavored. The other was cat food. "Um...I'd go with the white cheddar."

"*¿Que?* No, I forgot my glasses at the shop. I can't read this *para mi vida.* My Eddie, he likes those little fishy kind but I can't see which one it is."

Trying not to laugh, Miranda reminded herself that Lola wasn't a Velasquez anymore. She'd finally married Eddie Bishop after shocking the town by living in sin for two years. Miranda had always figured they did it just for the fun of fluffing people's feathers. Lola was that kind of woman. Or course, since her beauty chair was a more popular confessional than the one in the Catholic church on Mill Road, no one could afford to hold it against her. Unlike Miranda...

She took the two packages from the older woman's manicured hands and found the right bag on the shelf. She handed it to her and Lola took it with relief. "Maybe I should go get my glasses before I pick up his blood pressure medication, no?"

"Good idea," Miranda replied as a perverse thought blipped in her mind. "Otherwise he could end up with Edie Banner's birth control."

Lola laughed. "He could if Edie ever used any!"

Miranda clapped a hand over her mouth to stop her squeak of shock.

Lola must have mistaken her action, though, because she patted her shoulder and dug around in her purse. She came out with a lollipop and ripped off the seal. Before she knew it, Miranda had it sticking out from between her lips. "My youngest daughter is pregnant too. I keep these in here for her. Good, no?"

Blinking, Miranda could only nod.

"It gets better. When they start kicking, you might even have fun." Lola leaned forward to whisper, her surprisingly soft hand squeezing Miranda's arm. "Don't let these people get you down, *niña.* It's times like this, you learn who your real friends are."

"Times like this?" Miranda asked around the pop.

"No matter what they say, you keep your head up. *Tienes que tener orgullo en tu mismo.* Have pride. In yourself. In your baby, *especialmente.* It's never done anything wrong and neither have you."

That Lola knew about.

Lola shook her head and tsked. "I'm not just saying that. Your mother, she told me, you know. Your father used to have me come help her with her makeup. At the end."

Miranda's eyes widened until they hurt. She looked around swiftly, in case anyone was listening. Thankfully, no one was close

"It was too much to put on a young girl. She should never have asked it of you."

Miranda backed a step toward her cart.

"You did the best you could for her, *niña*. She knew that. She'd tell you now if she could. You don't have to punish yourself anymore."

"I'm not, I—"

"You deserve to be happy. She'd want you happy."

Her father wouldn't agree. "I have to go, Lola. It was nice seeing you again."

The expression on the other woman's face was sympathetic, which strangely hurt more than the whispers. As she passed the cart, Lola caught her by a hand to her elbow. Against her better judgment, Miranda stopped.

"People are saying some very ugly things right now. Things they have no right to say and I think you let them because *you* think someone *should*. That's not what your mother wanted to happen to you. She loved you. She was just weak. These people will forget, later, when your life is better. You'll have to let them. They'll forget what they say to you, what they say to each other, and they'll think you forgot too. You won't, but don't let it make you sour. You're a good girl and it won't always be this way. Believe me, I know. Once, no one in this town liked me at all. Now, they no care I'm the crazy lady with purple hair."

Miranda's smile was weak. "Because you know who you

are?"

Lola pffted at her. "Because I'm old enough to know everyone's dirty secrets. I go down, I'm taking those *pinche pendejos* with me."

Miranda couldn't help it. She laughed.

"People can only make you feel shamed if *you* let them." Lola patted her again "Thanks for the fishies!"

Then she disappeared into the dairy section, leaving Miranda with a box of cat food and a belly full of knots. She put the box down, but the knots refused to loosen as she wheeled her cart into the next aisle. At least she had the lollipop.

Lola proved to be the bright spot. Every time she passed someone, she either heard harrumphs or whispers in her wake. Some people had the graciousness to look guilty when she turned back to look, but soon enough, her patience ran out.

Like she was the first person to get pregnant in RDC. Or even the first person to have a complicated relationship. Hadn't Mae Belle and Jimmy Butner managed to carry on a clandestine affair for years? Edie Banner had four kids and not one looked a thing like the other, not a husband in sight. Well, all right, poor Edie got talked about plenty, but weren't there more important things to talk about? War? The economy? The fact that RDC had four bakeries and no fitness centers? *Something?*

She continued through the store, only to run into Hallie McCormick on the far end of the bread aisle. Miranda gave serious thought to spinning her cart around and running for it, but Hallie's eyes widened with the scent of a victim and she knew it would do no good. Hallie would run her down without even scuffing her bubble-gum-colored high heels.

"Miranda McTiernan!" The petite brunette put her hands on her ample hips and pasted a painful-looking smile on her face.

Hurrying, so as not to lose her prey, Hallie pushed her heavy cart until she was within inches of Miranda. The cart was filled to the brim with diet microwavables and ice cream. Yeah…that'll work.

"How dare you keep a secret like this from me?"

As if we were the closest of friends? Miranda thought with a sigh.

"Like what, Hallie?" She grabbed a jar of peanut butter she didn't need and began reading ingredients she didn't care about. Maybe if she sounded disinterested enough, Hallie would go away.

"Like you being *pregnant*! And I hear it's twins! You must be so excited!" The woman must have been a foghorn in a past life. "Why, when my sister called me and told me last night, you could've knocked me over with a feather. Not that I blame you for getting caught, but getting pregnant to catch a man doesn't work these days. Don't you know that?" Shrill laughter threatened to make Miranda's eardrums bleed. "Still, you never know, maybe even *you* have a shot. It's *Josh* after all, isn't it? Everyone knows he'd do anything for you but eat motor oil."

Wasn't that just a testament to undying love?

"But I wouldn't count on it, not with all the rumors flying around. The second he gets it in his head you might've gotten knocked up with someone else's kids, even Josh will be out of there, believe you me." She shook her head and popped a snack chip between her still moving lips. "Men just have no sense of chivalry anymore."

Hallie had the most amazing ability to be blissfully unaware she was insulting someone to their face. Either that, or she was simply that rude. Miranda couldn't decide which.

People can't shame you unless you let them. It was good advice. Made a nice mantra. Might even keep Miranda from knocking Hallie McCormick on her plasticky ass. Miranda put the peanut butter back on the shelf and set to leave. One could only turn the other cheek so far.

"Unless, of course," Hallie continued, tone coy, "the rumors are true. But that would just be so *wrong*. I told my sister, there's no way you'd do that. Miranda's not that kinda girl, I said. I mean, can you *imagine*? What kind of woman would you be if you tried to tie Josh down with Danny Randalls' kids? You'd be sick. Just sick. And we all know you wouldn't do something like that. After everything else you did to those two, that would just be too much."

The cart in Miranda's hands made a squeaking noise beneath her white-knuckled grip. She turned, glaring at Hallie who finally seemed to realize she'd said too much because her back straightened defensively.

"*That's* what the rumors are? You people actually think I'm having *Danny's* babies?" The horror of that felt like a punch to the gut. "What about his parents? Did any of you think about *their* feelings before you started spreading such stupid lies?"

Hallie didn't even flinch, which said more than enough about her character. "It's not just me, honey. Everyone's saying it. This whole town knows how you played those men off the other for years. Fact is, it's anybody's guess who the daddy is. Isn't it?"

Miranda remained frozen to the spot long after Hallie shrugged and rolled her cart past. This was so much worse than being called flaky. Or reckless. Or even brainless. People would look at the babies day in and day out, checking for some sign that they were Danny's. They were digging into the memory of a good man, a lifelong friendship, and turning it into something dirty. Something cruel. And, oh God, *Josh*... What would it do to him, to the way everyone in town looked at him?

He'd be called six kinds of fool for believing her.

If he stayed long enough to believe her.

"What's the matter, honey?" Hallie's sugary voice asked. Miranda turned her way, almost in a haze. Hallie wasn't alone anymore. Two other women, fuzzy faces with judgmental smirks, watched her too while Hallie giggled. "Feeling sick again?"

Miranda pried her hands off the cart, leaving it sideways in the aisle as she stalked to the front of the store. Maybe it was her imagination—she didn't know because she was struggling to see past the gathering tears in her eyes—but the air conditioning must have broken. Sweat turned her skin clammy. She pushed past people, ignoring carts and sounds because the doors were right there, but just like a nightmare, she felt like she wasn't getting any closer. All she could think, over and over again, was Hallie's question, *Isn't it?*

Why did her worst humiliations happen in this store? And why did she stay in a town where no one thought anything but the worst of her?

She skidded to a stop. Lola didn't think the worst of her. Trisha didn't. Even Josh didn't, at least, not in the same way.

They can't shame you unless you let them.

She looked around, knowing she'd made a spectacle of herself, all but running for the door. All around her, people watched curiously, waiting to see what she would do. Be the sad little sap who went running home, waiting for Josh to solve her problems? Or would she stand up for herself?

She was walking before she even realized what she meant to do.

The teen cashier gasped and pressed herself into a corner of the register when Miranda's hand shot out for the phone connected to the light pole. Having shopped here all her life, it didn't take much thought to press "#" and "8" to end up on the storewide intercom.

"Hey everyone, this is Miranda McTiernan. You know, the redhead you're all so busy gossiping about?"

Customers in the checkout line stared at her with eyes like owls and not so much as a squeaky wheel made noise. Good. They were paying attention.

"I thought I'd take a minute and set the record straight. Yes, I'm pregnant. Yes, I'm having twins. And yes, Josh Whittaker is the father. No, Danny Randall is not. Danny was my friend. He was a *good* friend." Her throat threatened to close up but she swallowed and pushed on. "And I am sick at the thought that you people, people he considered his friends, people who went to his funeral and pretended to care about him, to cry for him..." She couldn't finish. She didn't even know what to say.

Around her, jaws were slack, some heads turned away. Some folks pretended they didn't hear her.

Miranda shook her head. "I hope the day never comes when any of you find your heart broken. That *you* don't have to look up for a helping hand when the wildfires come this summer. It's people like Danny, people like Josh, who risk their lives every day, year after year, for *you*. And all you can do is talk about them like they're your own personal soap opera. So go ahead and talk. Make up your stories. If that's what it takes to make you pathetic people happy, go ahead. I just hope you can live with yourselves when it's *you* on spit." She slammed the phone so hard the feedback rang through the store. Spinning on her heel, she walked out and into the heat of the summer day.

She got all the way into the car before she realized she was still hungry.

ꕤ

"...idea if Josh knows. He's on duty. Stop laughing, Trisha." Miranda's voice drifted out of the kitchen.

Josh opened her front door wider, looking around for Rusty. For once, he was glad the moronic dog didn't bark. The golden retriever lay sleeping half in the tiled foyer, half into the living room on the right, sprawled on his back, upper body twisted to one side, hind legs spread wide like a mantrap—the very picture of way too much information. Not so much as an eyelid flicker. God, he had to get her to put in a security system. Or at least a deadbolt.

"No, I did not punch Hallie McCormick."

Josh shouldered his way inside, putting down the bags on the tile before pulling the key out of the doorknob. She didn't know he'd picked his key off her nightstand and while this might give it away, he didn't have much guilt. After carefully closing the door so as not to wake the snoring animal, he lifted the bags again and started through the house.

Unlike his own, her childhood home had more earmarks of her parents than herself. Except for the clutter—that was all Miranda. Fluffy-looking throws hung on the couch, books left on just about any surface, sticky tabs with inexplicable notes and color dabs flapped from windows, thresholds and bookcases. The pictures had changed only in that they were cluttered on shelves and surfaces beside more frames and faces. Her grandmother's old black-and-white in a pearlescent silver frame shared space with a plastic ladybug that had images of Trisha's three kids peeking out of the spots. It was crazy, haphazard and totally without any thought or order. But it was homey as hell. The whole house was that way As if Miranda lived on the surface of a happy mother's refrigerator.

Soon, she'd be the happy mother, too.

He hoped.

"No, I'm not calling him. What do you mean why? Because he's going to yell at me."

Josh turned from the pictures he hadn't meant to follow and crossed the foyer into the dining room. Miranda's mother's hopes for a big family remained in evidence in the form of the dining room table, a massive mahogany beast with a gleam that could blind. It ate most of the small dining room and Josh had to crab walk around the chairs. By the time he got to the swinging door of the kitchen, the sound of Miranda chopping something could be heard as well as her continued argument with his sister.

"I guarantee you he's not going to be proud of me. Josh is never proud of me."

He winced. He was always proud of her intentions. It was her methods that drove him up a wall. Maybe he needed to make that distinction a little clearer.

"Don't you have children to keep track of or something... Ha-ha, very funny. No, I'm not coming over for dinner. Thanks, but I can take care of myself, you know. I have food. *Somewhere*," she added softly.

Josh entered the kitchen, watching as she opened her pantry and stared inside. Cleaning supplies, some basic staples like mashed potato flakes and tomato sauce. Bin after bin of cereal. Pasta. Canned tamales that Raul would yell at her for owning. She sure seemed to like her cookies.

"I've got some," he offered.

Her shriek damn near burst his eardrums. The phone clattered to the ground as she spun around into the pantry shelves, gasping. She stopped hyperventilating after a second, her eyes narrowing on him. "What the hell are you doing?"

"Bringing your groceries?" Better to stick with the simplest answer. Anything else required more discussion.

"You almost gave me a heart attack."

"I wanted to surprise you."

Her eyes had yet to relax. "You wanted to make sure I wouldn't throw you out."

"Were you going to?" He moved to the counter and lifted the bags onto the cream-colored tiles. Without waiting for her response, he lifted out lettuce, carrots, milk, her favorite brand of cheddar cheese, low-sodium turkey. He heard her lift the phone off the ground with a grumble.

"Did you call him?" Even he could hear Trisha's responding cackle. "I'm so getting you back for this," Miranda said by way of goodbye. The beep of her hanging up rang in the silence. He could feel her gaze boring into his back. He kept pulling food out of the bags. Two jars of Alfredo sauce. Giant shell pasta. Popsicles. He heard her gasp when he pulled out the container of cut watermelon.

"How did you know I wanted watermelon?"

There wasn't much point in denying anything. "A little purple birdy told me."

She huffed, frustrated no doubt. Next thing he knew, she was grabbing the popsicles and the fruit to take to the fridge. "Just once, I'd like people in this town to mind their own business."

"You're in the wrong town, then. There's only twelve hundred people here. What else are they going to do but talk about each other?"

"I expected more from Lola."

"Actually, all she did was call to tell me you forgot your groceries. I grabbed a few things I knew you liked."

"You're telling me you left your shift just because I dumped a cart of groceries at the store?"

"No, I left my shift because Raul was tired of the lines getting tied up with people calling to tell me *why* you left your groceries at the store." Actually, Raul was laughing too hard by the third call. Within an hour, the firehouse had four visitors bearing edible gifts of appreciation and a donation toward the Firefighter's Widows Fund. A little schedule shuffling later, he found himself at the store, inundated with congratulations on his impending fatherhood. He lost count of the people who couldn't quite meet his eye.

"I didn't mean to—" The fridge slammed shut. "You know what, I did mean to. I'm not sorry, either, so don't expect me to apologize."

Josh turned from the food, picking up a grocery bag to fold. It gave him something to do with his hands other than reach for her. "You don't have to apologize. You didn't do anything wrong."

"Except make a scene."

"Some scenes need to be made." Considering what he'd done to Raul for just murmuring that the twins were Danny's, he'd have done a lot more than made some people ashamed of themselves.

"Oh." That was it. She hugged the watermelon to her chest, but her eyes lost that defensive look. Instead, the mossy green color was soft with vulnerability.

"Did you really think I'd be angry?"

She blinked slowly. "I always make you angry."

"Not always." He abandoned the groceries and started toward her.

Her eyes widened and she backed up a step. "You hate how

I'm always in trouble."

"But I'm glad I'm the one you call when it happens. Usually," he added because she hadn't called him this time. He'd make it a point to find out why.

"You hate my house."

"But I have a great time re-organizing it."

Her gaze shifted to his feet, which had moved him another step closer. "You can't stand my dog."

"He's the dumbest animal on earth, but he's loyal." Rusty was smart enough not to screw up a good thing. Josh apparently needed some lessons on the subject. In thirty years, he'd never managed to do anything but screw up what he had with Miranda.

"You think I'm a flake who can't take care of herself." She pressed herself against the shelves of the pantry.

"I think you're so busy trying to take care of others, you forget to watch out for yourself."

She stared up at him like he'd grown a new head. Maybe he had. This one with a brain. Then she swallowed. "You don't think I'm good enough to have your children."

"No, Randa." He sighed, reaching out to touch her cheek. He'd kept so many things from her. Too many. He'd always gotten past his conscience by telling himself she was better off not knowing. That she'd never find someone good enough for her if she knew how he felt. But all he'd done was hurt her. All he'd ever done was hurt her. "Whenever I let myself dream about kids, I never once considered having them with anyone else."

Tears filled her eyes, overflowing when she blinked, pained. "Then why?"

"Why what?"

"Why *everything*?" She grabbed his hand to keep him from backtracking this time. "Why wouldn't you be with me? Why have you always pushed me away? Even before—" She stopped herself, seeming unsure if she should continue. Or maybe unsure if he would stay to listen. Whatever she was worried about, it didn't stop her for long. "Even before I took those pills, you pushed me away. If my father hadn't died in that car accident, you might never have spoken to me again. Why, Josh?"

That hadn't been the plan. The summer after her junior year, something had shifted between them. She wasn't just Miranda anymore. Not just Trisha's best friend. Not the annoying little girl she used to be. Somehow, when he wasn't looking, she'd become something more. Something he hadn't been able to stop thinking about. When her mother got sick, she'd needed someone to lean on and he'd been the one she turned to. For a few short months, he'd been free to love her and dream of what the future might hold. Until the one night neither of them gave a thought to her curfew...

"Your father came to see me. After." He backed away and this time she let him. "He had hopes for you. Him and your mother both. You were going away to school. You were going to get an education. We both knew you, knew how you felt about me. He said you would stay, for me, for your mother, and he knew you'd never go back to school. You'd pass up all your dreams, all your opportunities. He didn't think your mother could handle you losing everything you'd worked so hard for. Thought she'd lose ground with her health."

"He didn't know she was terminal yet." Her voice was flat. Cold.

Josh shook his head, regrets she'd never know filling him, but at least the weight of them was familiar. "He was right and he was just trying to do the right thing for you and your mother. You didn't need to be fighting with him right then. I thought, later, we'd have the chance to be together. It would just be a few years. So I broke things off. To make sure you went through with your mother's wishes." She did. She even went to summer session, almost desperate to avoid him. She came home for the Thanksgiving holiday. A week later, her mother was gone. Davis McTiernan died in a car accident on his way to bring Miranda home for the funeral. but it was all for nothing. Miranda returned to the safety of her parents' home and never went back to school, just as Davis feared.

"Most of them, anyway," she replied, her eyes distant.

"What does that mean?"

She blinked, as if shaken from her reverie. A harsh swallow later, she crossed her arms around herself. "I loved my parents."

He waited, but when she didn't say anything he nodded. "I know. I remember."

"Sometimes, I think I forget."

He could only stare at her. How could she forget? This house was practically a shrine to them, lovingly preserved.

"I think we all forgot. She didn't want him to see her die that way. He was so angry to be losing her that he blamed me. He thought I gave her the pills she used to...to..." She made it a point to force him to talk about her own attempt on her life, but even now, years after Marie's death, she couldn't seem to say the words.

"It was the grief talking," he said, tone quiet as he could make it.

She still flinched. "Maybe. Or maybe it wasn't. All I know is in the end I lost them both. I've lost everyone and everything that ever mattered." Did she know she was pressing her hand over her belly? Or was she afraid this blessing would disappear too?

"I'm still here."

Her steady gaze met his. "Are you?"

He didn't falter. Not in this. Not when she needed him the most. "I'm not going anywhere, Rand."

He waited, breath held, for her to accept. He knew the moment it happened. She took a breath, slow and measured, and her lips curved into a shaky smile. "You promise?"

He cupped her jaw, pulling her into his arms and lowering his face into the softness of her curls. She wrapped her arms around his waist, burrowing into his chest before she sagged against him.

"I promise." He held her that way for a few minutes, grateful to have things right between them. It was a gift he hadn't expected even that afternoon.

If only he deserved it.

Chapter Seven

I've followed her for a week now. She's never seen me. Never noticed I was close enough to burn her with the still sizzling end of a match. That's the kind of woman she is. Confident. Absolutely sure all is right in her world. The husband is one of those perfect types who works nine to five, mows the lawn on Saturday, takes the kids to the park on Sunday after church. He doesn't yell at the little monsters who trail after their mother like ducks. No swinging backhands from him. Nope, just sugar-sweet domestic bliss, day in, day out. Like a fucking TV show. I haven't heard them fighting or yelling, not even when the kids are asleep, like everyone else does.

It's almost enough to make me hate her.

But I don't need to hate her to kill her. I just have to know how much he loves her. Will it haunt him to know she died because of him? That she died, writhing in agony as the fire sucks the air from her lungs and eats away at her skin. How long will she scream? I've wondered about it for days, running my fingers over the button that will end her life. With Randall, it was different. I had to push him. I could feel the heat of the fire. The choice was gone. But now I have all the time in the world. It's cold compared to that night on the warehouse. No adrenaline until I touch the toggle. It works every time and I just keep myself from pushing it. It wasn't time yet. She always has the kids with her. But today, today she's finally dropped them off with their grandparents.

Now it's just me and Trisha.

After this, Josh won't be able to ignore me anymore.

No one will.

ᴕ꙳ᴕ

Miranda stood in front of her mother's full-length oval mirror. Three months gone. Her belly distended slightly, but nothing like the pregnancy books showed. She felt like she swallowed a watermelon and looked like a walking pack of sausage links. She had no modest feminine bump. No, somehow, she'd swelled evenly from head to toe into some thick tube of pregnancy. Except her breasts. Those had gone from apples to grapefruits practically overnight. And the random bouts of throwing up warred with almost violent cravings for foods she'd never much cared for before. Especially not at the same time. Like vanilla ice cream followed by pickled radish.

The only benefit was watching Josh turn various shades of green in either stage. Once he figured out he could avoid the sounds of retching by keeping her from having an empty stomach, she found herself inundated with snacks of all kinds. And water. Half the melon feeling was from being sure she sloshed when she walked.

But she wouldn't trade the last month for the whole world.

Something had happened to Josh the night of the grocery store debacle. Oh, he still watched her like she was a ticking time bomb, but he didn't hesitate to touch her anymore. Not even in public—though even she knew there was no reason to since everyone and their grandma knew she'd been sleeping with him. More often than not, if he wasn't on shift, he had an arm around her. Or held her hand. He even rubbed her feet while they watched movies or did any other thing typical couples did. As if they *were* a typical couple.

It'd be heaven if it weren't absolute hell.

She loved being with Josh this way. Spending time together without arguing. Teasing that led to kisses and kisses that led to so much more. Waking up in his arms, laughing at the intimacy of lovers' jokes. But she hated fearing that any moment, he could turn to her and say it was over. That he still didn't love her and didn't think he ever would. Not that Josh would ever put it that way, but it's what he would mean under all the politeness. Her heart almost couldn't take the constant waiting. Almost. Until it absolutely couldn't, though, she was keeping her issues to herself.

They ate dinner together. They went on walks together. She did his laundry, he fed her dog. She made an effort to keep her house from swallowing him and he did his best to keep her chocolate stash from her. They made love whenever the mood struck, which was more often than she'd expected. If she hadn't been pregnant already, there was no doubt that she would have been by now. For all intents and purposes, they were any other married couple waiting for their first birth.

If she allowed herself, it would be so easy to believe the fantasy. That she and Josh could spend forever this way, not asking for anything more than this. That she could be happy not knowing when it was all going to end. In all the years she had halfheartedly wanted to be one of the women he dated, she had never imagined how heart wrenching the experience might be.

Live for the moment, Miranda, she reminded herself sternly. *Take what you can get and be happy, remember? Be happy, dammit.* She forced her mind to think of better things. Like the fact that she and Trisha and Penelope were taking a much-needed day off from kids and deadlines for some heavy-duty spa pampering. In twenty minutes, Trisha would pick her up and they'd do some serious damage to their bank accounts in the name of de-stressing. Miranda thought desserting would be a better idea, but a massage and a mani-pedi never did a girl wrong. And maybe when the day was over, she'd feel a little better about where she stood with Josh.

Wherever that was.

Dressing in a loose blue empire-cut blouse and soft black palazzo pants, she figured this was as good as it would get. At least the shirt gave the impression she *could* be pregnant instead of just tube shaped. Maybe she'd ask Trisha which maternity shops were the best. The sooner she made it obvious she was expecting, the less likely she'd find herself sobbing at not being able to find any pants that fit in regular stores. Plus, she could probably squeeze another day with the girls out of it. Nothing made shopping more fun than watching Trisha and Penelope argue over what was acceptable in public and what wasn't.

Finally, she heard the familiar sound of Trisha's mini-van pulling up to the curb. She was on the stairs when she heard the staccato beep-beep of Trisha's horn.

"Yeah, yeah, I'm coming." Not that Trisha would hear her. Or care, really. Once she was free of kids, Trisha turned into a speed demon without match and she would have no patience for the fatigue that made Miranda drag. The second horn beep came as she was opening the front door.

"Come on! We've only got six hours!" Trisha called from the van, half-leaning out the door.

"Bite me," Miranda mumbled, putting her key in the lock with a grin. Trisha was even less likely to change her ways than

Josh. Whittakers were just born pushy.

"Miranda!" Trisha whined, bouncing in her seat. "Hurry! I gotta pee!"

"Why not just do it here?" Miranda held open the house door for Trisha. "It's either two minutes here or an hour of scrubbing and a lifetime of mocking!"

It was probably the mocking that decided her. Miranda laughed as Trisha pulled on the handle, her shoulder yanking back while she groused with what could only be bad words she'd never say in front of her kids.

And then the world turned every shade of fire.

Miranda didn't hear the roar of the explosion until she was thrown backward into the foyer. Into complete black.

ଔଓ

"Bullshit." Raul, still buttoning the heavy yellow slicker, twisted in the front seat of the fire truck to look back at Josh. "You guys go up on the terrorist target list recently? Since when does RDC have bombs going off?"

"Probably a gas main or a water heater blew," Josh said, more to himself, securing his gloves.

"Dispatch is saying car bomb," replied the driver, Curt, over the sound of the wail. He turned the oversize wheel onto Elm, sliding the truck through the spare traffic of folks who couldn't figure out which direction to pull out of the way. The other four men in the cab were all set now, hats in place, jackets closed. The usual fine tension filled the vehicle while they stared out the window to get a bearing on where they were headed. Whose house they might have to lose.

The problem with living in such a small town was that when something went wrong, odds were you knew the person well. Went to school with them or someone in their family. Talked to them regularly at church. It made the job harder, but every single one of the men there was dedicated to doing it. This time, the only one with a sense of something seriously wrong, it seemed, was him.

Josh's frown deepened when Curt maneuvered onto Orange Glen. He turned back to Raul. "What's the address on this?"

Raul picked up the mic. "Dispatch, repeat destination, over."

"Two-fourteen Magnolia Ave, Fifteen. Multiple casualties, paramedics en route. Over."

His heart stopped. It simply stopped.

"Fuck." Raul growled, kicking the floorboard of the truck.

"What?" Curt asked, making the long turn into the arcing curve of Magnolia Avenue. The smoke billowing up from the street stained the sky and even a hundred yards away, Josh could smell the blackness.

"That's Miranda's house," Raul answered as Curt pulled the truck to a slow stop, but Josh was already shoving his way out of the truck. This was wrong. It had to be wrong.

His boots hit the ground and he began pushing past people—onlookers and arriving emergency personnel. The foul smell of burning gasoline stung his eyes and nose, foam extinguishers firing at the still-crackling hulk of an inverted vehicle. Black smoke surrounded it, but he didn't see her on the scorched curb or on the untouched porch. The house wasn't damaged that he could see, which meant she could still be in there. All his training told him to be calm. Be deductive. *Think.* But no matter how his brain screamed at him to use it, all he could hear was the pounding of his heart and the all-encompassing need to get to Miranda. Touch her. Hear her. Look in her eyes and make sure she wasn't hurt. It couldn't be her. It couldn't.

He spun around, searching faces and seeing everything and everyone but the one person he needed most. "Miranda!"

A few people turned their heads as the crew took more hoses to the flames still devouring half the lawn.

"Miranda!"

"Josh!" He heard Raul distantly. By the third call, he'd pinpointed him, expecting to find Miranda safe with him. Instead, Raul was coming to him, arms outstretched, a mask of concentration on his face.

No.

Josh wanted to look somewhere else, ignore the advancing panic, but all he could do was shake his head while Raul came ever closer. He knew that look. He'd felt it on his own face before, when he had to tell someone he knew that they'd lost someone. Sometimes the most important someone...

"Don't tell me this." If Raul didn't say it, it wasn't true. She'd be waiting in her house with that damn dog. Waiting for him to come and tell her it was all clear.

"You can't be here, Josh," Raul said, getting a hold of Josh's arms even as Josh backed away.

He shoved Raul off him. "Don't fucking tell me this!"

"She's en route to the hospital."

They didn't have one in RDC. All major incidents, from car accidents to births, were transported to nearby Poway, which had a full service hospital and surgical center. They could treat anything there.

He took his first real breath. "She's alive?"

Raul's expression was grim. "I'm not sure. Neither of them was conscious."

Multiple casualties. He jerked his head to the side, taking in the smoking heap at the curb. It hadn't occurred to him at first. Miranda drove a compact. Even flipped on its top, the back door blown nearly off, that was no compact. It could only be a minivan—

"Trisha." His insides shredded under a lash of agony.

Raul grabbed him, for the moment the only reason Josh could stay on her feet. He forced himself to focus. He'd be no good to either of them if he couldn't get a grip. He couldn't fail them. Not again. "How bad?"

"I don't know." Raul let him go, but watched him carefully.

"Raul, you gotta tell me."

"No, you gotta get over to Pomerado Hospital. When she comes to, she's going to need you." Which didn't sound good. Raul knew something. "Get a hold of your brother-in-law. He needs to be there. Just in case."

Shit. "You know something."

Raul's jaw worked. "I only talked to Tony for a second." Tony being the EMT remaining for any other emergent injuries. "One of them needs emergency surgery, they're transporting her to the nearest open space for a Lifeflight pickup. He said there were internal injuries. It was bad, Josh. It was really bad."

He closed his eyes. *Stay calm. Get to them. Get to them.*

"He didn't say which?" *God, he wasn't sure he wanted to know.*

Raul shook his head. "Go. We'll take care of this."

Josh stared at the nightmare that was Miranda's yard. Five hours ago, he'd stood in this spot and waved to her from his truck. Now she could be dying and there was nothing he could do.

Again.

Go. This time, he followed his mind, but in his heart...he remained afraid.

ঙ্গ

Miranda's first moment of clear thought was that there must be a thousand cotton balls in her mouth. Maybe two. Still, she ventured to open an eye. The piercing light made her shut it again. Determined to fight through the fog, she tried again and managed to keep it open long enough to realize the light was only the dim overhead fluorescent. Before her was a room she didn't recognize. Blankets on a bed she didn't know. Finally adjusting, she opened the other eye and blinked.

Beige walls with a thick painted border of pink caught her attention first. A table situated near the matching pink window seat boasted only a short coffee cup and a wadded ball of what must have been a wrapper. Wood floor. High bed. To her right a machine was monitoring something with a line that rose and fell in small molehill shapes. If she didn't know better, she'd think she was in a hospital.

She blinked again, this time taking stock of herself. Her head ached, her arm hurt and she felt like she'd been run over by a truck. Had she? She tried to remember what happened, but her brain remained fuzzy. Something...

No. Nothing. She just couldn't focus. Finally, she looked down to find Josh asleep at her side, slumped over her casted left arm, his hand spread wide and possessively over her belly.

She stared, eyes wide, at his hand.

The babies. Had something happened to them? What would make Josh reach out to maintain that kind of connection with them? She'd know if...if...

Summoning her strength, she lifted her right hand and gently rifled her fingers through his hair. He sat up immediately. Miranda gasped at his worried expression. His wide blue eyes were red and, unless she was mistaken, slightly swollen. Adorably wrinkled from what was obviously a long night, he rubbed his charcoal-stubbled cheeks.

"You're awake." Why did he look so surprised?

"Where are we?"

"Pomerado."

Hospital. Crap, she was right. "The twins—"

"They're fine. It was touch and go for a while, but...Penelope thinks they're going to come through okay. She wants to keep you for a few days, to make sure." He pointed to a machine that had a ribbon of paper slowly issuing forth. Numbers changed constantly on the screen. Plugs protruded from cords she belatedly realized were connected to an elastic belt wrapped around her waist. "It's a fetal monitor, so don't move around too much. They have a hell of a time finding the heartbeats." He smiled and reached a hand to smooth across her face.

She leaned into it and closed her eyes. "What happened?"

"What's the last thing you remember?"

She frowned, though it hurt, almost as if her face were bruised. "We had dinner last night. We went to sleep...you got up early for your shift. Me and the girls were going to have a spa day." The mirror. She'd been looking in the mirror...the horn. Trisha leaning out the window...unlocking the door and then... "Fire. It was loud. Hot." As if someone had come and thrown her into the foyer, the force of the blast pushed her into the wall. Her eyes snapped open in horror. "Trisha. Where's Trisha? Is she okay?"

Josh's lips tightened, his head bowing.

Panic clawed at her. She struggled to sit up, but Josh's

hand moved from her belly to her chest and kept her still.

"She's alive, Rand. I swear to you, she's alive."

Tears stung her eyes and her chest hurt for reasons that had nothing to do with keeping her still. "But?"

"She needed surgery. There was some shrapnel from the bomb—"

"What bomb?" Why would there be a bomb in Rancho del Cielo?

"Someone rigged one under Trisha's van. If it had been in the front or wired to the ignition, both of you would be dead." His voice strangled on the words. "As it was, you had some bleeding and you needed stitches on the back of your head where you hit the wall. We think you landed on your hand; your wrist was broken. Overall, you were far enough from the explosion that the majority of the damage was from the fall. Your internal organs don't seem to have any serious injuries."

But Trisha had been right there, stepping out of the van. "What about her?"

"Trisha needed her spleen removed." He blew out a breath, so slow it hurt her to see him stretch for control. "She has burns on her back. Scattered lacerations. Some torn ligaments in her shoulders and a broken jaw from the impact. They're keeping her sedated for the pain. Michael's with her."

"But she's going to be okay…right?"

The strain pulled any relief from his face as he nodded, rubbing the back of his hand across his cheekbone, repeating the swipe at the moisture from the other eye. "Tentatively, they're saying yeah."

But she knew he was keeping something from her. She tried to pick up her hand to touch him, but the cast was heavy and she still felt so drained. He must have seen the motion because he gripped her fingers.

"They'd had to restart her heart. EMS response was fast, but it was one of your neighbors doing CPR until they arrived. She should be fine but..."

"But you're not going to feel safe until she comes to."

The grip on her fingers tightened. He shook his head, bowing it down to the cast again. His shoulders shook and all she could do was reach with her good hand to touch his hair. Try to soothe the fear that had to have gripped him until he couldn't even feel that it had let go.

"You couldn't have known this was going to happen, Josh. You're not all-seeing."

His shoulder hitched with careful casualness while his face stayed averted. "Do you smell guilt or something?"

"No, but I know you. You'd find a way to be responsible for my allergies if you could."

"We should have been there faster."

"How? Teleportation? It takes nine minutes from the station to my house. I've seen you guys run the time trials all over town. You couldn't have gotten to us any faster than you did. And honestly, Josh, if you had been there when it went off, you could have gotten hurt too. You've got nothing to feel guilty about."

He raised his gaze, his blue eyes giving away a glimpse of what looked to be torment. "I've got more to be guilty about than you'll ever know, Miranda."

She swallowed, a frisson of fear sliding through her. She held firm nonetheless. "Not this."

He looked down again, his rough fingers touching her arm above the cast and at her fingertips. He didn't want to argue and she knew he wouldn't agree. She let the subject drop.

"How's Michael?"

"You know Michael." She did. A perfect foil for Trisha's brashness, Michael was sophisticated and calm. No matter what wild tempest Trisha pulled him through, the man never batted an eye. "He almost lost it when they told us the extent of her injuries, but once they said she'd be okay, he pulled it together."

"Trisha always says he wouldn't know what to do with himself without her."

Josh nodded. "For the first time, I think I believe her." He tried to smile at her, but his mouth wobbled and his eyes filled right in front of her. None of them would know what to do with themselves if they lost Trisha. Especially on the heels of Danny's death.

"It'll be all right, Josh. Trisha will be okay." Her voice shook, but she forced herself to steady. Trisha *would* be fine. Believing anything else wasn't possible.

"I know," he replied, his voice little more than a whisper. "It's just...I think about Michael and what he's going through. Waiting for her to be all right. Hoping nothing else goes wrong and I know it makes me a selfish bastard, but all I can think is how glad I am that it wasn't you."

Ohhhh. "It wasn't."

"But it could have been. What kind of bastard wishes this kind of pain on his own sister?"

She couldn't argue. If she hadn't been dragging, it would have been so much worse. She let her hand slip from him to her belly which was still firm, creating a small rise under the blankets. The babies inside her were still so small, but they'd impacted her life in ways she couldn't begin to count. If they lost them because of this, if they lost Trisha...

"But I don't know what I would have done if it had been

you." Heartache tore at her soul as she looked into his eyes.

"I know. That's exactly how I felt when—" She had to swallow what felt like a boulder in her throat. "When Danny died."

Josh stared at her, expression slack.

God, it was callous, but she had to explain. "Danny was my friend. I cared about him and it hurt so much to lose him. But when they said there was a firefighter down, I was terrified it was you. I'm *always* terrified it's you."

"You've never said anything."

"What was I supposed to say? Stop doing what you love? Stop being who you are?" She shook her head, stopping quickly when it throbbed in reminder. "People need you. You need to be there for them. I understand that. I've never had a right to ask you to stop and I wouldn't even if I did. If it means I hold my breath every time there's a fire... Well, at least I look good in blue." He didn't smile at her joke. She shrugged as best she was able. "That's just the price I pay, Josh. But it's always been worth it."

He frowned at her. "The price you pay for what?"

She stared at him, wondering if he truly didn't know. A warmth inside her gave her courage when she'd always managed to talk her way out of revealing too much. That bomb was nothing if not a warning. If—God forbid—Trisha didn't make it, at least she'd have lived her life with the knowledge that she'd given her entire heart to someone. That she'd been brave and that she was loved. But what did Miranda have? Years of near-misses and regrets. Words that were never said but always meant. She wanted more than that. Besides, if they weren't past hiding now, they never would be.

"The price I pay for loving you."

For almost a second, he didn't react. The span of that time, the moment between her heartbeats, she thought she might have reached him.

And then he winced.

Like a spell breaking, hurt snapped against her chest, forcing her to flinch in new pain. He blew a breath out, probably searching for some words that would comfort her. He'd be looking for a while because there weren't any. She wished she could pull her own words back in, but they were gone and she was exposed. Rejected.

Again.

She pulled her hand from him, curling the cast against her chest with her good hand. Josh let her go, face bleak. Without touching her, he didn't seem to have anything left to do with his hands. Or with himself. Long, empty seconds drew out. If she could move, she'd curl up and roll away from him, but the wound wouldn't heal if she did. She'd be trapped just as she had been all her adult life. It was time to get everything out on the table. Get over it or get on with it, as her father used to say when she was hampered by indecision. She didn't have anything left to lose.

"Why won't you love me?"

He sighed, shaking his head.

"You love me, Josh. I *know* you love me. Sometimes I've wondered—a girl kind of has to when the man she wants pushes her away all the time. But the truth has always been there, staring me in the eyes. It's why I could never get over you. You give me just enough to keep me hanging on. To keep me from really loving anyone else. It's not that you don't love me. It's that you *won't* love me and I want to know why."

Josh leaned back in his chair, still not looking her in the eye. "You're tired. This isn't the time or the place. You're supposed to be resting."

"I'm *supposed* to be doing a lot of things. I'm *supposed* to be at a day spa with my best friends, letting them comfort me because the man I'm in love with would give anything not to be with me." She shifted her legs away from him as well. She could feel his stare follow the movement, but he didn't stop her.

He only sighed again. "It's not like that and you know it."

"Really?" Her voice strained to reach the pitch and he winced at how high she managed. "Because you've explained oh so well?"

The noise he made could have been a growl. But it wasn't an answer.

She couldn't let him think it was. "Is it because of what I did with my mother's pills? Because you can't forgive me?"

She could have struck flint off his cheekbone right then and started a bonfire. But still he said nothing.

"Is it because I was involved with Danny? Because I was weak enough to need someone to love me?"

Watching him tighten up and turn away only made the hurt inside her worse.

"Because I hurt him by not being able to love him back?"

He finally looked back at her then, his gaze burning her like fire, but it wasn't nearly as stinging as her own conscience.

"I owe *him* the apology, Josh. Not you. If you want to hold something against me, go ahead, but not that. You don't have the right. You never *wanted* it."

"Miranda—"

But she kept going, unable, unwilling to hear anything from him but the truth. "Is it something else?"

"Miranda!"

"I need to know why, Josh. *Talk* to me! Tell me why can't we just love each other." The childish part of her wanted to pick at him with it until she got some kind of reaction. A word. An excuse. A lie. Anything but this awful silence. "Why is it so damn hard to forgive me?"

"Because it's not about forgiving *you*."

Her voice caught in her throat, stuttering while he surged to his feet. Every line of his body taut with anger, he swiped at his leg before crossing to the small table near the far wall. He braced his hands on the curved edge. She could only watch and wait for him to find the words to explain.

"I *failed* you that night, Miranda. You needed me, I knew it. I could see it on your face but I left anyway, because it was ripping me apart to see you hurting so much and not have the right to comfort you. You were still angry at me for the way I broke up with you. I couldn't explain about your father the night you buried him. And I couldn't take the rejection I knew I deserved. I put myself first and you almost died because of it." The table legs made a faint screaming noise on the linoleum as he shoved it roughly toward the window seat.

"Josh." She breathed his name, her anger bleeding out at the same time.

"I could have lost you that night. I couldn't forgive myself then any more than I can forgive myself now. Nothing I do is ever going to change that."

"What about what *I* do? What I need *now*? Doesn't that matter?"

He lifted his head, not to look at her, but as if looking up to the sky for help. "I'm here for you, Miranda. I'll be what you need—"

"I need for you to love me. Wholeheartedly. Without regrets or guilt. I need you to let me love you back." But talking to his back, she couldn't know for sure if she was reaching him. Not until he shook his head. She was so frustrated, she could have happily flung something at him to knock some sense into that subtly moving target. But there was nothing in the room except the two of them and the secrets they carried. "*I* was the idiot who thought I had nothing left to live for. I let my grief and my guilt get the better of me and it almost cost me everything. But *you* saved my life. It doesn't matter that you left. All that matters is that you came back, Josh. That's all that ever mattered to me." Didn't he realize? How could someone so intelligent not be able to understand? "There's nothing to forgive."

"No, I never should have left you alone. You were fragile and scared and grieving and I still left you to deal with it by yourself." His voice shook with pent-up anger. If he could have crushed something, he probably would. He'd fight anything for her, she knew that. But when it came to fighting himself, he had no idea when to stop.

She forced her voice to calm. Screaming at him would only harden his resolve. "I know what it is to blame yourself for things you couldn't control. My father blamed me for my mother dying and I blamed myself for his death. But what good did it do? It doesn't bring anyone back. It doesn't take away the pain of losing them. It just eats at you until you've got nothing but regret piled on regret. We finally have a chance to start over, Josh. To start the life we should have had years ago." She reached her hand out to him, kept it up so that when he turned, he'd see it. Would know she was offering everything she had inside her. "Take it."

The rigid line of his spine didn't change, didn't relax. The seconds ticked away until she finally let her arm drop. Nothing she'd said made a dent. She accepted it, finally, and let the last pieces of her heart break apart. Made herself do what had to be done.

"Then if you won't be with me, if you can't bring yourself to love me, you need to go."

He spun around then, vivid eyes bright with anger even though her voice had been so soft she'd barely heard it herself.

She answered his glare with as much calm as she could muster. "I want to be loved, Josh. Not tolerated. Not begrudged. And I refuse to be the weight you keep tied around your neck."

"You're not—" He spilled a deep breath, pinching the bridge of his nose and squeezing his eyes shut. His "gathering patience" pose. She would have laughed if she could find so much as a molecule of humor beneath her pain. "I knew we shouldn't be trying to talk about this right now. You're upset about Trisha, you're tired, you're hurt—"

"No matter how many excuses you give me, I'm going to feel the same way tomorrow and the day after and the day after that."

His mouth tightened into a hard line.

"All this time, you've been telling yourself I'm a flaky airhead so you could justify everything you do for me. So no one would realize that you love me and you need a way to stay in my life. To have some kind of say about what I do. And I've played into that. I've been your damsel in distress, coming to you to save me from myself, just for the crumbs of affection you were willing to give me.

"Well, I'm done, Josh. I'm done twisting myself into what you need because you're too much of a coward to reach for what you want. What you *really* want. No more lies, no more schemes, no more bending to your decrees. If you can't give me what I need, I want you to go."

His eyes narrowed, catching on something while she spoke. "What lies?"

Her heart skipped a beat. It was one thing to claim courage. Something else entirely to find it when you needed it most.

He took a step toward her. “What lies, Miranda?”

She put her hand over her belly, as if to protect them from the truth. His eyes followed the movement. He took one breath, two, his gaze never wavering. Not until they lifted to meet her own, too incredulous for rage. He knew exactly what she’d done.

“You weren’t having fertility problems, were you?”

She hugged her belly tighter. “These children weren’t conceived because of that.”

“For the first time in your life, Miranda, tell me the damn truth.”

As if Josh would know the truth if she kicked him in the face with it. But she gave it to him anyway. “I asked Penelope about artificial insemination and she said if I wanted it, putting it off very much longer might lessen the chances of success. She explained how to monitor fertility cycles and I seriously considered it. I almost went through with it. But...”

“But you came and lied to me instead.”

She refused to feel guilty. “If you’ll remember, you didn’t care about my ‘condition’. You said no.”

“You *lied* to me!”

“I had to!” She caught herself, pulling back on her volume before they attracted a nurse. She glanced unsteadily at the monitoring machine. The numbers didn’t change drastically, thank God. Just slightly larger molehills. She turned back to him, determined to get it all out while she could. While he was still there to tell. “You would never have touched me if I had just asked you, ‘Oh, hey Josh, I know you won’t consider a relationship with a nutcase like me, but do you think that we could just have sex? Just on the off chance that I could get pregnant?’”

“Enough with the drama,” he ordered, but she couldn’t do

it. The secrets needed venting.

"Because I can't take being without you any more."

"Stop."

"I just wanted one piece of you that was mine. Oh!"

Suddenly, he was there, grabbing her arms, forcing her to look him in the eye. "I said, stop it, Miranda."

She stared up at him, wanting so much for everything to be different. But wanting had never changed anything. She'd always had to initiate change herself. But what had it gotten her? Heartache after heartache. And now she felt as if she were ripping those torn pieces of her heart out completely because this was the change in her life she'd never wanted.

"I didn't plan for all of this to happen," she whispered. He might never believe her, but it was true. "The night Danny died, I was so sure it was you. I don't know why. I just knew that it was and that everything we never got the chance to say or do or be was gone. But it wasn't you. It was Danny. And as much as it hurt, as guilty as I felt, I couldn't spend one more day wasting my life *waiting*. I had to do something. Change everything. So I came up with my stupid plan. Thought out everything, hoping to God I could just make you look at me again. The way you do when you forget how crazy I make you. I never thought you'd want me for anything more than a night. I didn't even think you'd want me for that long."

"I've always wanted you, Miranda," he admitted, his deep voice resonating in her ears, his gaze pained. She could see regret in his eyes. Understanding the man you love didn't always mean you could handle what you found in him.

"But you won't be with me. Not in the way I need you to be."

He shook his head.

"Because you just can't manage to forgive people, not even yourself."

He let her go, his hands sliding down the length of her arms. Lingering, but letting go all the same.

"People make mistakes, Josh. It's human nature. We don't learn without them." A final plea. A last line of reasoning he might accept.

"I know. In my head, I know...but when it comes to trusting people, I can't do it. I look in their eyes and I see every slip-up they ever made. It all adds up and I can't let it go. I just keep waiting for them to do it all again. When I'm with you, I can't even think beyond the next minute. I never see the road ahead. How can I protect you that way?"

As if she were some kind of prize someone was going to steal, or a target anyone would aim for. She was just the bane of his existence. Everyone knew that, except maybe Josh. "At least I wasn't the only deluded one in this relationship."

"What's that supposed to mean?"

"It means I don't need you to protect me. I never did. What's to protect me from? I live in a small town, I write children's books, for God's sake. The person I talk most to in the world walks on four legs and clubs me with a tail. Yes, I get into trouble sometimes"—she paused at his snort of disbelief—"probably because I'm on my own. The real truth is I make mistakes that you can't take back. So you make all kinds of excuses so you can keep looking at me. We're *both* liars and I'm sick of it. We shouldn't have to lie to each other just to be together." She wrapped her blanket tighter to her body, watching him process her logic.

"Babies make mistakes, too. Did you think about that? They take forever to learn things. They fall down and they don't listen and they get hurt no matter what you do. You have to be able to forgive them, too. But you won't be able to do that, will you?"

His gaze flickered, as if he had to think about it. He actually had to think.

"You have to go, Josh," she whispered, so let down she could barely breathe. Heart broken. Pride gone. The least he could do was leave her her dignity.

He stood there, towering over the bed, looking at the beeping machine as if it were going to give him some answers or the right words to say. Finally he did as she asked, silently and without complaint.

Dignity didn't mean a whole hell of a lot when he slipped out of the room.

Chapter Eight

The bitch didn't die. Something either went wrong with the relay switch or I was late on the button. I haven't decided which. The only consolation is seeing the guilt on Josh's face. This finally hurts him. His sister surviving in pain might actually be the better option. If I want to, I can drag this out for months, carving a tiny piece of her away, one bit at a time. By the time I'd be done with her, there'd hardly be anything left of poor little Trisha.

But she's not the one I want.

I wander through his house undisturbed, touching things, wishing I wasn't wearing gloves. I want to feel the textures. Leave my mark everywhere. Stain it the way he's stained me. The house is quaint. Old, but sturdy. A big Craftsman. A lot of families probably grew up here, kids as happy as bobble heads. There's not much around to read. The few shelves are full of old knickknacks and manuals. One looks like a liquor cabinet. Big fuckin' surprise there. Wouldn't be a Whittaker house without a place of honor for the booze.

The furniture is nicked in a lot of places. Like it's been here for years. I pick up the corner of a newspaper left on the dining room table. It's from three days ago, which means Josh hasn't been home in a while. All the better for me.

He doesn't leave things out of place much. I knew that

about him already. Some people let their guard down in their own home, but not Josh. For a second, I wonder if he keeps things neat for the same reason I do. Because he remembers what happens to you if you leave a toy in the wrong place. Put a glass too close to the ledge. Touch the wrong thing at the wrong time. It wouldn't matter to me if he does. If he wakes up at night, still afraid, then I'm happy about it. It's no less than he deserves.

The faces in the pictures aren't the one I'm looking for, but they'll do. I collect them as I move through the living room. His mother. His sister. His best friend. Strange thing, though...not one picture of Miranda. I bet that really bothers her. Makes her feel unimportant. It should. He'll wish he had at least one when I'm done.

The upstairs ain't much to grin about either. Plain wood floors, same as down below. White walls, bathroom at the end of the hall. One open door leads to a bedroom. Two closed ones probably are bedrooms too, never used because Josh's house is too big for him. It's a place where happy families should be. But they aren't here. Whittakers don't do happy families.

The open room has a big dresser, a long rectangular mirror hanging above it. The bed is made, the dark blue comforter pulled smooth over the surface. I dump the pictures I found on it, enjoying the wrinkled mess. But there should be more. Inside the drawers I find his clothes. They go next on the pile. The closet holds uniforms, dress clothes. Boxes labeled with words like "receipts" and "records". Nothing marked "personal". Not much means anything to Josh. I grab the uniforms and throw them on the bed with everything else.

Yes, this will do.

I pull the old flask from my pocket. It's one of the only things I've kept with me no matter what. Silver, engraved with lines and grooves that lost their relief over the years. It used to be the picture of a hunting dog running through high grass. Now it's just lines and grooves. A ghost of what it used to be. Like me.

I open the top and pour out the fluid onto the pillows, over the stack, into the comforter. The scent is strong, revolting. I almost threw up filling it, but emptying it on all of Josh's things keeps the gorge from rising. When it's empty, I throw it on the pile, too. He'll recognize it. He'll know this is all about him, now. He'll know he deserves this.

I pull the matches from my pocket. The fire breathes to life in my hand, small and desperate. It needs more than the skinny match to keep it alive. I intend for this one to burn long and slow. Babying it, I cup my palm around it and lay the match next to the small puddle of bourbon on the uniform sleeve. Then I sit back and watch. It doesn't take long. The flames begin to rise, crackling and rumbling as it tastes this and that. Soon it begins to savor. Curling edges of fabric, blackening pictures inside frames.

I sit still and I watch the things Josh loves burn away into nothing.

Soon, it'll be his entire life.

ଔ

Josh dragged himself inside his own house to get his duffel bag. Thoughts of Miranda evaporated as soon as the door opened and the smell of smoke slammed him in the face. He looked up at the smoke detector above the door, but its smashed hood hung off the ceiling, ready to fall.

He knew he should back out, call for the crew, especially after what happened to Trisha, but he moved forward anyway.

It didn't feel like a fire. No building heat. No straining of the wood expanding. He knew better than to just rely on instinct, but everything about the stale air said "cold". Even the sense of menace felt more like an echo.

Moving room by room, step by careful step, he checked the downstairs and finally, the up. Tension ran out of him at the sight of his bedroom through the open door. His bed had burned. Torched, then extinguished. The water still dripped onto the floor. The closet and the dresser drawers hung open, showing emptiness within. That would explain part of the smell. That plastic/wool singe scent that stung the eyes. The other part, though, was a smell he'd avoided for years. One that had been out of this house since he was six years old.

Bourbon.

His father smelled like that, sour-sweet, regardless of whether his glass was full or empty. Almost as if he wore it.

Josh almost shook off the old memory. Almost. Except his eye caught the glint of silver amid the charred remnants of his dress coat. Blackened by the fire, the grooved lines of the old design looked just the same as when he was little. The last time Josh had seen it was the last time he'd seen his father, seventeen years ago.

Jared had appeared virtually out of nowhere, knocking on the door while their mother and stepfather were gone shopping. Trisha had answered, a fourteen-year-old girl staring at the haggard stranger she probably barely recognized. But Josh recognized him instantly. Hard to forget someone when they haunt your nightmares. His face had deeper lines, grayer tones, his hair gone gray in more places. Underneath, it was still the face Josh hated seeing a resemblance to each morning.

Jared had come there to ask for forgiveness, not that he got a foot in the front door. He held out the empty flask to prove he was serious about drying out. He even blathered on about how he'd remarried and how he'd made a new life up in Santa Barbara. Josh didn't listen long. He made Trisha go to her room and told his father to go to hell. Jared stuck around a while, wheedling for them to talk to him through the front door. As always happened, though, he lost his temper. Soon he was pounding, demanding they to pay attention to him. The entire time, Josh leaned against the door, determined to keep it shut, once and for all. Each rocking blow on the wood rattled against his spine, shaking the cold sweat just the sight of his father had created, but he'd stayed there anyway. Eventually, Jared had left, taking that flask with him.

Now it was back. On the burned remains of his bed. The day after someone tried to kill his sister.

Messages didn't get clearer than that. For some reason, Jared Whittaker had chosen now to come back into their lives. And it didn't look like he wanted forgiveness this time around.

Josh turned on his heel and rushed out of the house. He was already dumb enough for one day, staying inside when there'd clearly been a fire. He had to call Raul. Get the sheriff's office involved. He shook his head, imagining what his home might look like once the technicians were done dusting, printing and searching for whatever the burglar had left behind. Then, whether she liked it or not, right to get rid of him or not, he was going to stay with Miranda until he knew for sure that she was safe. Jared wouldn't get through the door again.

First things first, get to his cell phone.

"We got a problem," Josh informed Raul once he was behind the wheel of his truck, his cell pressed to his ear. He started the engine with one hand and made quick work of his U-turn to head back toward the main road.

"Yeah, no shit," Raul grumbled, sounding as if he were

chewing on something while he talked. "I'm looking at the preliminary report on what was left of Trisha's van. We got a *big* problem."

"Someone broke into my house and set a fire in my bedroom."

The silence from the other end of the line could only be called edgy.

"I think it was my father." Josh pulled into traffic on the main strip, willing the other cars to move faster. The highway entrance two miles away could have been light-years for as fast as he was moving. Finally, he was on the old two-lane back road, no one ahead to care how fast he sped.

"I thought your dad was dead."

"He was to me." The truck ate up the miles, but it was still interminable minutes ahead of him before he hit Poway city limits. "You need to get a hold of the sheriff. Trisha needs security."

"I did that yesterday. She's had a guard since we verified the explosive. That's what I've got to talk to you about. The bomb was triggered by a short-range signal. Extremely short-range. The sonofabitch had to have been on the same street when it went off. He had to be watching."

Jared Whittaker. So close to them that he'd waited until Miranda was within range...

"I'm already on the way back to the hospital. Get someone on Miranda's room."

"Josh, there's more." He heard the rustle of papers as he finally saw the sign for his exit ahead. "I wasn't called down here just because Danny died. I was called down here because there's been a suspicion of a serial arsonist. The county chief wanted someone who could fit in and dig out information."

"You mean he suspected one of *us*." Someone from his own squad, starting fires all over their town? It wasn't possible.

"Not necessarily. He needed me to rule you out."

You. Not the crew. Mind racing, Josh turned onto the off-ramp, and pulled to a stop at the waiting signal. The red light forced him to stop and think. It didn't take much to guess what Raul was getting at. He hadn't thought much about it at the time, but no one wanted him to have any information about the forensics of the fires lately. He'd just assumed they didn't want him brooding. But what if it was something else? "He thought I started the fire that killed Danny, didn't he?"

"I'm sorry, man." Raul sounded it. "Prelims said it looked electrical, but Old Man Richards had that barn rewired last winter. There were overload blocks. As soon as an outlet fried, the system killed the line. The smaller fires on the ground level were set, not sparked. And they found tool marks on the roof. Whoever did it went after Danny on purpose. The chief had to consider you."

Josh gripped the wheel, almost sure he could feel it bending under the pressure. "You know I wouldn't do that."

Raul snorted. "I knew that when they called me. But if it was true, I wanted to be the one to bring you in. I owed Danny that."

Josh didn't bother asking why. Danny had a connection with just about everyone in town. Their boyhood friend probably owed Danny as much as Josh did. "Why are you telling me all this?"

The pause weighed on Josh's chest, rendering him unable to move the truck and get where he needed to be.

"Because I know you'd rather have fallen through that roof yourself than watch Danny die. And because I saw your face when you realized Trisha was hurt. Whatever's going on, it's bigger than anyone thought. And if your father is the one behind it—"

"He is."

"Then you're the only one who's going to be able to figure out where he's headed next."

Not bloody likely. Even at the age of six, Josh hadn't seen eye-to-eye with Jared. He'd never be able to guess out his pathological reasoning. No point in telling that to Raul now, though.

"When you call the sheriff, have him run down my father. He has a record. It won't be hard." Josh hung up the phone, wanting like hell to scream at someone, to rip the whole truck apart with his bare hands. Danny. Trisha. Miranda. Who was next? How far was Jared planning to go?

He forced himself to close the anger off. Shut it down along with the rage and the guilt that threatened to swallow him whole. There would be plenty of blame later, when Miranda was safe.

He jerked the truck into gear and drove down the road toward town. Toward Miranda.

ଓଃ

The opening door of her hospital room didn't hold the silhouette Miranda was hoping to see. In fact, it was one she'd been ducking since the funeral.

"Hi, Mrs. Randall." *Please let her think the frog in my throat isn't guilt.*

The tall blonde's smile looked sincere, if sad. Danny had taken after her a lot, Miranda noted, as she always did whenever they crossed paths. His same friendly green eyes, the thick honey-blonde hair. The dimple at the side of her mouth.

She and her husband were outdoorsy, to say the least, and it showed in their strong physiques and the casual athleticism of their son. Her years in the sun had put lines on Jennifer Randall's face as well as a tan that seemed to have seeped down to the bone. She'd never been unkind, not once, not even after the breakup, but still, Miranda hadn't had the guts to face the disappointment on the woman's face another time.

"Hello, Miranda." Jennifer walked on silent feet to the side of the bed. Her eyes swept the area for cords, followed their path to the monitor and its attendant screen. It stayed there for a few seconds, as if Jennifer were apprising herself of the babies' condition. "Is that good or bad?" she asked, pointing at the screen.

Miranda followed her finger to the scrolling bell curves, however slight they'd gotten. The nurse had tried to explain that the curves were uterine contractions and that they were considerably fewer and of less concern than when she'd arrived. But no one would tell her how bad that had been.

"Honestly, I have no idea. They aren't telling me much other than I shouldn't move. Or get upset," she added, thinking of the argument with Josh and how the nurse had rushed in with a shot afterward that could have doubled for a six-shot espresso. *Don't get upset, but let me hype you up with something that feels like you just jumped out of a plane. Yeah, that made sense.* "No one's rushing in, so I guess it's okay."

Jennifer nodded. A minute passed with nothing but silence. Finally, the older woman cleared her throat and looked Miranda in the eyes. "I—I haven't been sure what to say to you since..."

Miranda nodded, her aching head throbbing a little at the motion. Since the funeral, where Jennifer could hardly look her in the eye.

"Since Danny broke up with you."

Miranda could only blink. "You—you knew about that?"

A small smile tilted Jennifer's lips, only adding to the list of resemblances. "Danny and I were close. He knew I'd keep it to myself. I've always wondered though, why you wanted everyone to blame you."

Miranda looked down at her hands, her good one picking at the raw edges of the cast. "People loved Danny. I didn't want them to think less of him." Which was true, but not all of it. Her throat grew tight and tears she never wanted to shed in front of this woman stung her eyes. "And I guess I wanted some shred of pride for myself. It's bad enough people think I'm an idiot. Can you imagine if I was suddenly 'the woman no one wants'? It was selfish, but Danny didn't mind."

"Oh, I'll just bet he didn't," Jennifer replied, her tone dry.

Miranda didn't like the way that sounded. As if Danny had taken advantage when it was the other way around. So much of her wanted to beg forgiveness of Jennifer, but even if she did, it wasn't the other woman's to give. Pointless as it was, she still choked out words that would have as little comfort as the endless platitudes from town. "I never meant to hurt him."

"Oh, honey, I know. We all knew." Jennifer reached out, taking Miranda's fingers away from the cast with a maternal pat. "Especially Danny."

Miranda lifted her head so fast it made her vision blur. "What?"

Jennifer met her gaze, startled, but seemingly determined. "Danny. He was never angry with you for what happened. He knew exactly where the blame was."

With Josh, probably. Miranda's insides tightened at the thought of Josh feeling responsible for Danny's lost dreams. He didn't deserve that. "Mrs. Randall—"

"That's why I came here. I heard what happened over the

scanner—"

"You have an emergency band scanner?"

Jennifer's shrug said "of course" for her. Miranda had one too, but only because Danny furnished it so she'd know they were all right. Plain reason should have told her he'd do the same for his mother. "I came down as soon as you were cleared for visitors. I couldn't put it off anymore."

"Put what off?"

"The letters." Jennifer pulled her purse across her belly, reaching in the aged brown leather and coming out with two white envelopes. "Danny left these. In case anything happened to him. He wrote them about a month after you split and kept them in his apartment. I found them when I was cleaning it out for the next tenant. There was one for me, too," she added, her sad smile brightening.

"He was always the kind to think ahead. With his profession, he knew any fire could be his last. Every six months, he wrote out what he felt might be significant—messages, instructions, that kind of thing—and put them in his safe. We had a standing promise that anything important would be in there and I would take care of anything that had to be done."

Miranda stared at the extended envelopes, unable to believe Jennifer expected her to take them. The top one had her name written in the familiar block lettering. Danny always preferred printing, so there'd be no mistakes about his intentions. And because he hated how flat his cursive turned, the bane of his left-handedness.

"Please, Miranda. He wanted you to have them. I should have given them to you weeks ago, but I...well, I don't really know why I put it off. Fear, I guess. Maybe a little bit of shame."

Startled, Miranda turned her gaze from the letters,

incredulity straining her voice. "Why would you feel ashamed?"

Jennifer's lips trembled as she tried to maintain the weak smile. Finally, almost relieved, she let it go. "He was my son. I wanted him to be happy and he'd loved you all his life. Someday, when your children are grown, you'll understand how much it breaks your heart to know they're hurting."

Maybe it was the concussion, but Miranda couldn't follow what Jennifer was trying to get across. "I don't know what you mean."

"*I'm* the one who encouraged him. I told him he was letting his own sense of honor or his friendship for Josh get in the way of his right to be with the person he loved. Convinced him that maybe the reason you couldn't seem to get over Josh was because you didn't have any other options."

Miranda clapped her hand over her own mouth when she sputtered with unexpected laughter.

Jennifer brightened at the sound. "You have to admit, that much was possible."

Miranda finally found a smile that wasn't bittersweet. "Yeah, it was, I guess." To anyone looking in, her love probably looked like a crush that just never went away. Jennifer had no way of knowing the bonds she and Josh had forged. All anyone ever saw were their struggles to break them. "I just...never saw anyone else."

Jennifer's face froze a little, making Miranda feel guilty all over again.

"I did love Danny. We all loved Danny. I never wanted him to get hurt," she repeated, but it sounded as weak now as it had before. "I just wanted him to be happy. He deserved so much more than I could give him. I tried to tell him, but he just said what we had was enough for him. Until it wasn't." Until she broke his heart by caring too much about Josh's anger. "You have to believe, if there could ever have been anyone else, it would have been him."

Jennifer nodded, looking down as if to hide her tears. She wiped them away with a brusque swish of her fingers before lifting her head again. "He knew that. He knew you tried. It just wasn't meant to be." Jennifer laid the envelopes on Miranda's lap with a small pat. A final goodbye, Miranda supposed. "Please take them. There's one for you, one for Josh. I'd give it to him myself, but I think he's hiding from me the same way I was hiding from you."

Give Josh a letter from Danny? Miranda almost asked Jennifer to take it back, but the woman was already on her way to the door.

"He'll come around eventually, so please tell him he's always welcome. Just because I lost one son doesn't mean I have to lose the other one I spent so much time raising. Besides, his mother would never forgive me." Jennifer put her hand on the handle, ready to escape, but then stopped. She looked over her shoulder and Miranda held her breath in response.

"For a short while, Danny *was* happy. He had you and he had hope and for just that little bit of time, he was happy. I know things didn't work out the way he wanted, but for the rest of *my* life, I will always be grateful." Jennifer pulled the handle and the door swung open. "You be happy, too. That's what Danny wanted most."

Then she was gone.

Miranda stared down at the envelopes. They might as well be burning a hole on her lap. She wanted to brush them off. Hide them away, so they'd stop sitting there like rectangles of accusation. Not that Danny was the kind of man who'd use his last messages to loved ones as an opportunity for hate mail. But still...

Be happy. As final wishes went, Danny hadn't exactly given her an easy assignment. True happiness was the one thing in her life she'd never been able to scheme or will or make happen. Maybe she was selfish—who was she kidding, of course she was selfish—but she'd always been happiest with Josh. She'd gotten by okay without him. Her hopes of a career bringing happiness to children across the country had come to life. Her dream of bringing that joy to children of her own had nearly come true, too. She could live and live pretty comfortably without Josh. But still, she wished it could be different.

She curved her hand around her tummy. In a perfect world, she'd have married Josh years ago. Her mother never would have gotten sick. Her father would have walked her down the aisle, they'd have had kids who were spoiled absolutely rotten by grandparents on both sides. Trisha would be fine. Even Penelope would be happy, with a father for her daughter and at least one person letting her live down her childhood crush on Raul. Danny would be alive, married to the right girl, hugged half to death by all those kids he'd always wanted. But the world wasn't perfect. The world was a place where you took what you could get and made the best out of the rest. The world sucked.

Leave it to Danny to expect her to make more of it.

"Uncle Danny is out of his mind," she said to the swell under the blanket. "We'll be okay. There's nothing wrong with being content. Most people don't get that much. We can do this together, can't we?"

There wasn't anything definitive from the curve under her hand. In a few more weeks, probably, she'd be able to feel kicks and touches. For now, the babies were definitely giving her the silent treatment.

"Well, we will. We'll take care of ourselves, just like we planned in the beginning. We'll take on the world together. Our own little family. You, you and me. We'll travel if we want. See new places and try new things. You'll go to school where I went to school. You'll be smart like mommy and pretty like Daddy. And when you grow up, you're going to have all kinds of choices in front of you. *Your* choices. And nothing is going to hold either of you back. Not guilt. Not fear. Not even love. Mommy will always support you. And Daddy—"

Just then, the door swung open, Josh all but sliding in, out of breath and looking desperate.

Well, well, well. Speak of the devil.

Chapter Nine

"Was that Jennifer Randall coming out of here?"

"I don't know." Miranda's mouth twisted into a smirk, her eyes narrowing as she pierced him with a glare he knew he deserved. 'Why don't you go after her and find out."

"No." Josh closed the door behind himself. Adrenaline still coursed through his veins, hot and rushing. For some reason, he'd expected to come into the room and everything be different. Changed by the knowledge that there was a threat. But her security hadn't even arrived yet. He'd only been gone for forty minutes. The only thing different was that instead of dealing with a hurt Miranda, he was facing an angry one.

"Get out, Josh."

He eyed the monitor. The line remained nearly flat, meaning he wasn't creating the havoc he had earlier by letting her make her ultimatums and demands. "No, we have to talk."

"We've already talked," she reminded him. "You suck at it."

This was precisely the reason he usually gave her days to cool off. If she had her way, they'd argue for the sake of arguing whether or not they'd argued. They had neither the time nor the energy, either of them, to go in those kinds of circles. "I know, but that's not what we have to talk about."

"What could possibly be more important than our future?

Or rather, our lack of one."

This was not going to go over well. "You're in danger."

It took her a full ten seconds before she started laughing, a bitter sound that should never have come out of her mouth. "It took you an *hour* to come up with that? Did Raul help?"

Josh gripped the back of his neck hard enough to keep his temper in check. "I'm serious."

"Sure you are." She rolled her eyes and slumped into her pillows, seemingly exhausted by her own anger. "Go away, Josh. Go see Trisha. Go to the firehouse or something. I don't care. Just *go*."

"You don't understand—"

"Tell me about it."

God would forgive him for shaking her, wouldn't he? "The bomb wasn't just meant for Trisha."

She finally quieted, her mouth closing slowly.

When he was sure she'd listen, he continued. "It was meant for all of us."

"What do you mean *us*?"

"Me, Trisha, you...the babies."

Her gaze snapped down to her belly. When it lifted back to meet his, her eyes were cloudy. "What are you talking about?"

He told her. Explained about the break-in. The flask. Even managed to drag out the last time he'd seen his father. The whole time she said nothing. It wasn't like her, really, not to interrupt, which meant she must be taking him seriously. After imparting the little he'd gotten from Raul, he waited for her to respond.

"So one more time, you're here to save me."

Not quite what he expected. "I'm here to protect you."

"Until someone from the sheriff's office comes."

"Until we find him," he corrected. Until he could see for himself that his father wasn't a threat to anyone. Especially not Miranda and his children.

"No." Her words were quiet but he could hear the steel in them. Crap. She didn't take that tone often but when she did, it never meant anything good for him. "You can stay. Outside. But as soon as that guard comes, you have to go."

Emotions roiled in him, pushing at his control like fizz in a bottle. "I tell you that you're in danger and all you can think about is some stupid ultimatum about our relationship? Are you serious?"

She had to be. She was back to the cold expression of zero tolerance, her eyes slitted and her mouth hard enough to chip glass "It wasn't an ultimatum. It's the way it has to be. If I give you an inch, you'll take the rest of my life."

Josh couldn't decide what made him angrier—that she relegated him to some overbearing bastard or that she wasn't listening to him at all. "I came here for you, Miranda. Because I care about you. Not because I want to own you or take you over. I have *always* been here for you."

"And you've never let me forget it, have you?"

Frustration he couldn't release raced along his veins like trapped fire. "Being angry doesn't give you the right to twist our relationship into something it wasn't."

Her gaze flickered. She turned her head away. Disappearing again. She couldn't walk away. Couldn't hide. But she could ignore him.

"And you say *I* have issues," he snapped, refusing to talk to the side of her head. He circled the bed to stand in front of her. "At least I'm here, facing our problems. Your answer is to just cut off anything that doesn't go your way, like some damn three-year-old kid."

And be as sullen as one too. Her eyes shot daggers at him. "I have a right to protect myself."

"Sticking your head in the sand isn't protecting yourself, Rand. It's taking the chickenshit way out. Your problems are going to be there when you come out."

"Maybe they will," she replied, tone acidly sweet. "But you won't be."

He crossed his arms. At least making her mad kept her talking. "You're so sure about that?"

"You never have been before." She lost the bulldog set to her chin, but her gaze remained dark and full of resentment. "All I've ever had to do was let you have your way, wait for you to get scared and leave. Works every time."

"Scared?" He almost choked. He glanced at the monitor. A tiny wave began to build in the line. Shit.

"Scared. Oh, you'll swoop in and save the day, sure. That's your job. But as soon as real life comes in, you're gone. Terrified I might start to think you'll stick around or something. Then you take off, telling yourself how noble and self-sacrificing you are when really, you're hiding just as much as I am. The difference is, when you go, I'm the one who's left to deal with everything. So don't tell me I'm acting like a child for not wanting to get hurt by you again, Josh. Not until you're prepared to stick around for once."

She said it all looking him dead in the eye, too. Did she see the color seep from his face? Feel that she'd struck home? It was the quiet times, when he could almost be happy, that all the doubts snuck in and stole his peace of mind. She'd always known?

"Do you remember what you said to me that night?"

He almost asked which night, but half a heartbeat later, he knew. The night she'd locked him out of her life.

"You couldn't even make love to me without warning me that it was only for one night."

He could tell by her face how much that had hurt. She probably knew it was the only way he could allow himself to give into the hunger that had threatened to immolate him, but she'd never said anything. Never stopped him. She just pulled inside herself, warding off the rejection until she could deal with it alone. All the while, he'd selfishly convinced himself he could have those stolen moments to comfort her. He didn't even realize he'd said the words out loud. Now, he could only wish words existed that would take the pain he kept inflicting away. But they didn't.

"What am I supposed to do, Miranda?" he asked tiredly. He couldn't give her what she wanted. He knew his limitations.

She shrugged, looking weary. "I've spent my whole life waiting for you to love me tomorrow, wanting you to love me today. And you don't want me to love you at all, but you won't let me go. Our lives are passing us by while I wait for you. There has to be a point where we both stop asking each other for the impossible."

He wanted to answer her, wanted to tell her it didn't have to be impossible, but he didn't know the answer yet. A last look at the rising swell of another hill on the monitor told him this wasn't the time to decide anything. He shook his head at her and moved to the door.

"Josh!"

He stopped, looking back over his shoulder. Probably too much to ask that she'd smile at him.

She didn't. She held out a white envelope. "Jennifer brought this for you."

"What is it?" It couldn't be good. Jennifer Randall and her husband might have been a second set of parents to him, but they couldn't be thinking very pleasantly of the man who'd wrecked Danny's chance at marriage. What if they thought the same as the county chief, that he had something to do with their son's death? He couldn't take looking in her eyes and seeing that. An envelope with the message wouldn't be much better.

She shrugged. "You'll have to read it, I guess." At his expression of distaste, she had her first moment of genuine mirth. "It's not like you have anything else to do out there."

Grudgingly, he snatched the envelope and escaped the room. After grabbing a chair from the nearby waiting room, he parked himself in front of the hospital door, back to being angry as the wood settled shut behind him.

Locked out, again.

He sat there, brooding over her words. She had a few points. But she was wrong on other things. Never been there before, his ass. He was *always* there. Always the one to catch her when she fell. Always the one she came to when crap hit the fan. Always the one who protected her from herself.

And then what?

His conscience had a strange sense of timing. It generally waited to ask pertinent questions until after he'd dug himself a hole. Sitting in that chair, firmly outside of Miranda's acceptance, he fought the obvious answer to that question. But there was no hiding from the truth.

She was right. Time after time, he'd get her back on her feet and then he'd go back to the ease of his uncomplicated life. Be relieved to return to his routine. Or at least tell himself he was. Allow her to steer clear of him for a few weeks, let her reset her inner expectations. Or maybe he'd used that time to reset his own while she saw the distance between them as another rejection.

Shit.

Looking over his shoulder, he tore open the envelope in his hands absently. She'd probably screech if he went back in and Penelope would have his head on a platter. Not to mention upsetting her meant risking the twins further. Even for Miranda, he wouldn't do that. So he turned back to the letter now open in his grip.

And instantly wished he hadn't.

So, I guess this means I'm dead.

Danny. Josh recognized the writing as well as his own. His heart clutched tight and his stomach stung with a sharp, breath-stealing pain.

I know you're tempted to ball this letter up and throw it away, but do me a favor and read it, okay? It's not like I can call in any of the other favors you owe me, right? And you know you owe me.

No, he couldn't. And Danny was right, there were plenty. Danny had been the "people person" of their pair. Josh had been too exacting, too demanding of himself and others, for many people to give him a second chance on their own. Danny had always smoothed the waters until Josh could make friends with them. To say nothing of the other ways Danny had saved him on a regular basis. As good as Josh tried to be, Danny was always that little bit better, faster, smarter.

Knowing you so damn well, I'm pretty sure you won't be at the funeral. And that you'll avoid my parents, even though they love you like you're their own. Which means you probably won't drag your ass over to the reading of the will, either. God, that sounds so uppity. Like I had tons to bequeath to people. Don't worry, you won't miss much. Mom gets my toaster. Dad gets my signed Gretzky jersey. (Sorry, I know you always wanted that, but he is my dad. Plus, he never pulls this girly silent treatment shit you do.) I left Miranda my convertible because, let's face it, that's one redhead who needs to be in a convertible and we both know I only bought it to impress her.

True, though Miranda hadn't said anything about it to him. Did she even know that shiny red dream car was hers?

Your sister got my baseball card collection. With any luck by the time her boys go to college it'll put a good dent in their tuition. You, my friend, to you I leave my prized 3PO.

The action figure? Josh actually put the letter down long enough to chuckle. Their friendship had almost ended over that damn toy...when they were five. They'd put their allowances together to buy it, supposedly to share. Josh had even put together a schedule that included alternating months and leap years, if he remembered correctly, because his mother had laughed about it. Of course, neither one had wanted to give the little gold man up. In the end, Josh let him have it, just so they'd stay friends.

We never did learn to share, did we? I think it's safe to say I was the problem, and I'm not just saying that because I'm dead. It's true. I've never been able to settle for second best in my life. Because I'm an honest guy, I'm gonna admit that I consider that my best quality. Except when it comes to you.

Or maybe just when it comes to Miranda.

Josh stopped reading. For a few seconds, he'd allowed himself to remember being a friend instead of being so angry, so...jealous, and it felt good. Light. Holding onto all those hurts got damn heavy some days. If he could just find a way to let it all go.

He'd been able to handle Danny being better at things—at everything, really—but he hadn't been able to take Miranda choosing Danny, too. He might have been able to live with it if she'd picked anyone else. Maybe. That she'd been about to marry Danny made it so much worse.

So who was he really angry at? Danny or Miranda?

She'd accused him of making excuses for her. Had he been putting it all on Danny? The idea was enough to shake him into returning to the letter.

I'd like to say she came to me. God, I wish I could say any part of our engagement was her idea. But I went after her. You know how she is. She hates to hurt people's feelings and I made it impossible to say no. I tried to tell myself she'd thank me someday. That I'd make her happy—happier than she'd ever been—and it wouldn't matter that I'd manipulated her into being with me. That I'd betrayed you and our friendship because I couldn't let go of the one thing I wanted most. Not until it was too late anyway.

Josh frowned. Miranda had broken the engagement. Hadn't she?

Scratching your head, aren't you? If I were still around I'd let you sweat it out, but well...there's only so many pages I figure you'll stick around to read.

It's not my proudest moment, but when people got it in their heads that Miranda had broken up with me instead of the other way around, I didn't correct anyone. I'm not sure why, but she seemed to want it that way and I owed it to her to leave it alone. Maybe you can ask and find out for the both of us.

Josh didn't have to ask. He and Miranda had the same problem—they both took failure to heart. If Danny had been the one to break off their relationship, she'd see it as someone else she hadn't been able to satisfy. Someone else who found her lacking.

"Danny, you dumb ass." Not that Josh had been

particularly brilliant about saving Miranda's feelings, but even he, insensitive shit he could sometimes be, knew better than that.

I guess the guilt finally got to me. I might be a greedy bastard, but I'm not a heartless one. Every time I looked in her eyes, all I ever saw was how sad she was. How damn hard she was trying not to wish she was with you. Knowing that nothing was ever going to be the same, not between us, not between the two of you. It can really make a guy feel like shit after a while. I realized that no matter how much I wanted her, no matter how much I loved her, one simple truth meant it was never going to work.

She's in love with you, stupid.

Josh laughed, a strange choked noise it took him a second to recognize came from his own throat.

If you haven't put it together yet, moron, you're in love with her too. I've wondered a few times if she only said yes to me thinking it would get your attention. If she did, it really worked. I've never seen you so mad, and I was there when Trisha went joyriding in your car all those years ago. Well, good. You finally figured out you could lose her.

Take a lesson from someone who knows—life is not long enough for you to go wasting it feeling guilty or unworthy about stuff you can't change. If there's one fact that won't change while you're on this earth, it's that you will never be worthy of Miranda McTiernan. Neither of us is, but you especially. You're ugly as hell. I've met wild animals with more charm. And you carry a grudge like a freight train.

But the difference between my unworthiness and yours is that she chose you. She's always chosen you. It just took too long for me to admit it to myself. But when I did, I let her go. If you're reading this letter, I'm dead a little sooner than I want to be but I can say this with my whole heart—I hope you're the one to catch her. She's everything good about you, Josh. So stop trying to make up for every wrong thing you've ever done on your own. You can't. But I'll tell you how you can make everything right. Pay attention okay, because this shit is golden. It'll change your whole life for the better and if you don't take this advice, you absolute prick, I'll come back and haunt you. You ready? Okay, here it is.

Marry her. You can't undo what you've done, but you can make it up to her. Spend the rest of your life dedicated to making her happy. See to it she spends the rest of her life smiling or laughing or something very close to either one. Because if she's happy, man, who gives a rat's ass about anything else? I guarantee you, you won't regret it. You might even think back on me with a little bit of gratefulness.

Well, all right, I'm dead, not delusional. Just trust me, okay?

Trust him. Josh shook his head. Trust didn't come easy—at all—most of the time. Was it all a simple matter of looking for a loophole in his own code? But it was a feasible option Josh had never considered. His own happiness with Miranda and their children would be a side benefit looking at it that way. Danny should have been a lawyer. Better yet, he should have mentioned this solution a long time ago. Josh sighed, a stupid grin on his face. Only Danny could point out the obvious and come out looking magnanimous.

I guess that about covers it. I'm not good at apologies. Probably worse than you are at accepting them. And I do owe you one, but I can't bullshit you on this. One just ain't gonna be forthcoming. I'd have to be sorry to pull it off and no matter how much it hurt, I'm not sorry for a single second I got to spend knowing she was mine. Even if it was all a lie.

Chalk it up to another one of those favors you owe me,

okay? Then give all the rest to Miranda. Poor kid is gonna need them if you ever do right by her.

The letter wasn't signed. It didn't have to be, but Josh stared at the final line until it blurred, wishing there were at least one more word. One more piece of his friend he could hold onto. Just like that, the knot in his belly loosened and faded away. Anger dissipated, leaving behind only a void of loss.

He rolled his eyes with the heel of his hand, pushing the hot moisture toward his temples. But more kept forming, the tightness in his chest building to a pain that felt like a thirty-pound weight between his lungs. By the third swipe he had to admit he was crying. Mourning. The bastard had finally got him. "Never should have dared you, should I?"

"Mr. Whittaker?"

Josh looked up to find a tall deputy in the familiar green and brown of the RDC Sheriff's office. He knew the kid. Twenty-four, at most, but armed, which was reassuring. Not commenting on the strange fact that Josh was sobbing silently into his own hands when he'd arrived was even better. The name came at him like a shot. Benny. Benny Rodriguez. His parents had bought their house from the Aldertons down the block when Benny was a kid. When had he grown up? Miranda's point that time had kept going while he stood still struck home again.

"Captain Montenga said you'd be here."

"Inside or outside the room?" Josh grumbled, hoping his face was clear of any remaining tears.

The kid did a bad job of hiding his grin. "Outside."

"Yeah, well, Raul's a smart guy." Too smart, the bastard. Josh stood, refolding the letter carefully, clearing his throat to get his emotions under control. He eyed the door, needing to go inside. But Miranda had made herself clear, and his reasons for not pushing remained—the twins needed protection first. "Let her know I left, will you?"

The kid took a look at the door, his gaze sliding back to Josh carefully. "Sure."

Josh stayed in place for a second longer. He belonged in that room. He belonged with her. When she was strong enough, when he was sure she was safe, he would be. Danny was right. Miranda was right. The past needed burying, finally. And when he got free of it, free of Jared, he'd let her know. For the time being, he'd have to leave her direct protection in the hands of someone else.

But not for long.

ঔ

Two days. She'd waited two days in her hospital bed and not a peep from Josh. No frustrated blustering. No growled demands. No silent glowering. Not even the emphatic apologies she deserved.

Though if she got those, she'd have to blame the concussion. The only positive thing to happen was that Trisha had come to with what looked like full faculties. She had a long road of recovery ahead and for the time being could only have limited visitation, but it was relief nonetheless.

"You look pretty miserable for someone escaping this place," Penelope said from the foot of Miranda's bed. She'd crept in while Miranda was ruminating and now stood there making notations on her chart.

Miranda scrounged up a smile.

Penelope raised an eyebrow.

So much for that. "Not buying it, huh?"

"Honey, I'm not even reaching for my wallet." The chart closed in Penelope's hands with a small clack before she tucked it under her arm. She smoothed the space at the end of the bed before dropping onto it with a sigh. Even with her white coat, she looked the same as she had as a kid, leaning sideways onto one elbow, head supported by her hand. They might as well have been giggling and eating snacks on Miranda's bed at home fifteen years ago. Sadly, the topic wouldn't have been any different.

"He hasn't even called," Miranda mumbled.

"Who, Josh?" Penelope's face scrunched into a rare frown. "He's called me more times than I care to count, checking on you and the twins."

Miranda stared at her, mouth falling open.

"I thought he was calling you too, then calling me to see if you were telling him the truth."

Miranda closed her mouth at that. It was too possible for her to doubt.

"He's been holed up at the firehouse, helping with the investigation. You didn't know?" When she didn't answer, Penelope's gaze sharpened. Being mother of a ten-year-old did wonders for her personal radar. "What did you do?"

"Nothing I shouldn't have done years ago." Miranda crossed her arms as best she could and turned her head to glare at the silent phone.

"Which was?"

Technically, there wasn't any reason not to tell Penelope. As a doctor, she was sworn to silence and as a friend, she should have Miranda's back unconditionally. Problem was, Penelope had that annoying sense of right and wrong that never failed. "I told him I want more from him. Like an actual commitment. And that I want him to accept me and the babies as we are, without him correcting us all the time. He wouldn't, so I told him to leave us alone."

Penelope whistled, a long rising note of impressed musicality. Normally, Miranda got a kick out of her preppy, perfect friend's habit of whistling like a poolhall shark. Today, not so much. "I'm guessing he took that about as well as he does your other ultimatums."

"Oh, *way* better," Miranda grumbled. "He walked out."

This time, the raised brows lacked musical accompaniment. Then she shrugged her shoulder and sat up, back to business. "So what are you so put out about?"

She couldn't be serious. But Penelope showed no signs of knowing the obvious. "Because he *left*," Miranda enlightened her.

Penelope remained unimpressed. "Sounds like he did what you told him to."

"Since when has he ever done that?" Josh did exactly as he pleased. Listening to Miranda generally fell somewhere on his to-do list between *sever own foot* and *ask for directions.*

"Maybe since you ended up in the hospital for concussive shock and a serious fall while pregnant with his children?"

Miranda sucked in a breath, which sounded like scraping leaves in the silence. Leave it to Penelope to make him sound rational. "Fine, take his side."

Penelope's laugh didn't soothe Miranda's nerves in the slightest. "You can't get mad at someone for doing what you tell them to."

Didn't she get it? Miranda didn't *want* him to leave. She wanted him to stay. To say the things she needed to hear from him. To be the man she loved instead of the ass she put up with. How hard was that to understand? "I'm pregnant,

Penelope. I can do whatever I want."

"True," her friend replied evenly. "You did what you wanted. Congratulations. I hope you're very happy with the results."

Sometimes, it really sucked having a friend who could say what she meant without saying anything you could get mad at her for. It was cheating as far as Miranda was concerned. But she didn't mention it. Penelope had heard it all before and it never once made a difference in her tactics.

"He probably just wants to give you some time to heal," Penelope finally said in her firmest doctor voice. The one that sounded all-knowing and impossible to doubt. "Calm down. Wait to talk until the babies are out of danger—which they should be, provided you take it easy and relax for the next few weeks."

"Weeks!"

"Yes, weeks. Just because you don't need to be holed up here at the hospital doesn't me you get to go cartwheeling all over town. Multiple pregnancies are touchy and your body has already had a shock."

Shock. That was a subtle way of putting it. "I can't just lie around for weeks, Pen. I'll go insane."

Penelope remained unfazed. "The complications multiply along with the children because your body is being taxed just carrying them and compensating for the drain on your resources. You don't have to be an invalid, just rest frequently and don't add any undue pressure. Take it *easy*."

"So you won't have a cow if I run to the store for something real quick?"

"I don't see why not, provided you're not up very long and you're not lifting anything heavy. If you notice any contractions, I want you to lie down immediately. If you feel four in an hour, call me. I don't care how slight, you call." Penelope waited for an admission of understanding. When she got it, she continued with a smile. "You might not believe it, but irrational fights and running around like a madwoman can wear a girl out. I'm guessing Josh knows that and acted accordingly. He'll get over whatever you said. He always does."

Sure he would. Because, 'get out of my life, you make me miserable' probably wouldn't stick in his memory. Miranda shook her head. "You don't understand. I can't just change my mind on this or blame the hormones. I was right to make him choose. He made the wrong choice. He always makes the wrong choice when it comes to me."

"Maybe. Maybe not." Penelope must have sensed Miranda's impending screech of betrayal because she added, "Maybe you did do the right thing. Just at the wrong time. And maybe Josh did the wrong thing at the right time."

"What are you? A fortune cookie? How can it be the right time to do the wrong thing? That makes no sense at all."

Penelope's expression clouded with something Miranda couldn't define. "You'd be surprised."

"What's that supposed to mean?"

Her friend shook herself briefly, her calm tones finally registering some irritation. "It means jumping a guy about your relationship in the midst of an emotional and physical crisis while his sister is in a coma could be considered a little unfair, don't you think?"

"No." *Yes.* Damn it. She scratched at the stitches in her scalp and winced. Maybe it was better when Penelope wasn't so blunt. Well, crap. "I wasted a perfectly good argument, didn't I?"

Penelope only smiled that serene nun-looking grin of the unattached. "I probably wouldn't use it in the next one if I were you."

"You sure there's going to *be* another one?" Josh had left, so angry she'd been able to see it coming off him in waves. Normally, she'd give him weeks to cool off. Or do something he'd have to forgive her for.

Except *she* didn't need forgiving this time.

"How about you save your hard thinking for home, kiddo. I don't want to have to explain all the wailing to the nurses. I brought all your paperwork with me and your nice officer friend is going to take you home and play guard until the sheriff gives the all clear. If you're extra nice to him, I'll bet he won't even say anything to anyone when Josh comes to grovel at your pudgy feet."

Yeah. Right. Officer Benny had a CB strapped to his shoulder. If Josh showed up at her house, the gossip might as well be mainlined. "They're not pudgy."

"Give it a week. In a month you won't even recognize them. If you can still see them, that is. Multiple moms grow exponentially. You're already carrying as much baby as a singleton at six months. Believe me, there won't be a part of your body that won't be pudgy soon."

Miranda glared at her friend. Like she didn't have enough problems to think about. "Have I mentioned lately how much I don't like you?"

"If not, you'll bring it up at delivery. In the meantime, go home, rest, don't push yourself, and if Josh shows up, you don't have to go back on your demands. Just give him a chance to talk. He might have something good to say."

"Josh?" The man who couldn't stop discussing neutering her dog?

"Do you really want to spend the rest of your life wondering what he might have said if you'd just taken a second to listen?"

Miranda's gaze skittered to the drawer of her bedside table. Did she want to spend the rest of her life wondering what

Danny meant to say, too?

No, but she couldn't read it now. She needed to be alone. Safe. It would wait a little longer.

"He'll come around," Penelope continued, oblivious to Miranda's guilt. "A man doesn't hang around for thirty years because he hates you."

"I never said he doesn't love me. He...I..." God, how do you explain the motives of a moron? "It's complicated."

"With you two, it always is. Which means, it'll keep until later. Right now it's time to get up. This place is for sick people, not certifiable ones." Penelope didn't stop bothering her until Miranda was sitting in a wheelchair dressed and reasonably prepared to go home. The flowers and gifts that had been delivered over the last few days—surprising Miranda more than anyone else—were loaded by a nurse onto a cart to be pushed behind her.

Officer Benny dutifully led the way down to the front doors. He'd made an almost decent card player while Josh stayed out of the line of her fire, but the poor kid would get eaten alive at the firehouse. Before long, he had her back to her house, where a huge black stain marred the street and curb and half her lawn was an overturned pile of dirt. Her car still waited in the driveway, the same as it had the day of the explosion.

Strange. Looking at the street and the burned grass, you'd think she lived in a war zone, but twenty feet away, the house remained untouched. As if nothing had happened instead of everything falling apart.

Benny helped her up the steps, not saying a thing when her hands shook as she unlocked the door. When the keys rattled right out of her grip, he bent to pick them up and undid the locks for her. Miranda hugged her arms around herself, rubbing warmth into the limbs despite the fading summer warmth. She heard barking from the backyard and smiled. Rusty.

"Do you want me to let him in? Your neighbors have been watching him for you, but I heard he didn't want to leave his doghouse in your yard."

More than anything, she wanted to hug her dog, but if she let him in, he'd trample her with his exuberance and Penelope would probably count that as a bad thing. She went through the kitchen to the doggie door he'd outgrown two years ago. He could still get his head through and half of one leg, which would have to do. She undid the lock and instantly his big golden head pushed through with piercing barks and the squeals Josh always compared to a three-year-old girl.

She rubbed his face with her own, laughing and scratching his ears while his eyes all but rolled back in his head. Finally, she had to shove him back out and let Benny help her to her feet. She washed her face and hands in the sink with a sigh. At least Rusty would always be happy to see her. But even his warm welcome couldn't quite banish the fear inside her.

"I can stay in the room with you if you want," Benny offered once she was sitting on her couch, staring out the picture window to the yard ahead. For some reason, being in her own home made her skin crawl. She wanted out. Wanted to be someplace truly safe, where simply looking out the window didn't fill her with fear. Where she didn't expect a wall of fire to blast into her face. If she could, she'd go to Josh's house. Hide in his big bed and bury her face in his pillow. He'd probably let her, if she called. But she didn't want to call. She wanted him to call.

God, when had she become such a *girl*?

"That's okay, Benny. I'll be fine." She could make that lie in her sleep.

"In that case, there's already been a preliminary check of the premises, but I want to give the outside another once-over. Just to be sure it's all clear."

"All clear for what?" Dread filled her belly as she knotted her fingers in the throw lying across the back of the couch.

"Any thing out of the ordinary," Benny said casually. He didn't mean it casually, though.

"You mean another bomb." Something else lying in wait, ready to explode in the blink of an eye.

Benny smiled. "Like I said, the fire department's been over this place with a fine-tooth comb. And the bomb squad. No one found anything. Don't worry. I just want to go over the property and check all the locks inside and out. It's procedure. I'll be right back."

She nodded, her grip tightening until it hurt as the young officer walked around her living room, checking on windows, before moving onto the kitchen. She listened for sounds of him working his way around, tracing him from one room to the next.

"I'm going outside now," his voice echoed from the kitchen. "Call out if you need anything."

What she needed was not to be here.

Cold splashed into her blood stream. How could she not want to be in her own house? She'd grown up here. She'd fought tooth and nail to hang onto it after her father's death. She'd stressed and fretted and yes, even fumbled at times. Desperately hanging on, needing to keep this place where their memories could be found in every nook and cranny.

The niches on her closet doorframe, her height, ticked off by a deep pen groove with her age written beside each line. Whenever she grazed her fingertips over the old wood, she could almost feel her mother's hand making the mark just above her head. Almost smell the soft perfume her mother wore. If she closed her eyes, she could see the vibrant red of her hair and the open affection of her smile. Her father's den, full of the books he loved, scented with sandalwood and citrus from the years he spent there, writing his novels. Tears pricked at her eyes, but she refused to let them fall. The rooms that years ago her father had, under duress, painted pink. Pillows and quilts her mother had designed and sewn. The worn carpets where they'd walked. The creaky stairs they had climbed every night on their way to bed. This very room still had the same wallpaper that Marie chose and put up herself twenty-five years ago.

The only place Miranda had rearranged was her mother's sewing room. Gone was the machine she had never figured out how to use, as well as the carpet that had needed to be destroyed long before her mother ever brought it in. Now, it touted hardwood floor, a sleek rolling chair and all her art supplies.

All those years ago, she'd stared at the overwhelming evidence of her father's financial situation—strained to the hilt from her mother's long illness—and feared losing the only home she'd ever known. It had taken more nerve than even she thought she possessed to call her father's agent and see if he could put her in contact with a children's publisher who might be interested in the watercolor illustrated stories she'd put together over the years. The man had been as good as his word, though, and sent her into the arms of an agent who'd taken her half-formed notion of an illustrated book about the squirrel family in her backyard and helped her shape it into Hazelnut the Squirrel, a character that had saved more than her house. Having purpose, having somewhere to pour her heart into had saved *her.*

Josh always told her to do something different with the house. Paint, rebuild, knock out a wall or two to modernize. Anything to make it her own. But she hadn't wanted to. She'd left the memories on purpose, usually wanting to surround herself in the family that was long gone so that she couldn't dwell on the fact that she had nothing else. Today, the memories calmed her when nothing else could.

Jared Whittaker had tried to take away so much more than just her and Trisha's lives with that bomb. He'd tried to steal her sense of safety, of peace, in her own home. She couldn't let him do that.

She lived here. Worked here. Had rebuilt her life here. He wasn't taking that away. She wrapped the blanket around her shoulders and lay back into the cushions, determined to stop being afraid. Her gaze met the bags Benny had left near her, the roses from Josh's mother peeking up next to the violets from Lola Bishop. Next to them, unobtrusive but eerily present, waited the white envelope Jennifer Randall had dropped off. The nurse must have packed them all together, not realizing Miranda half-hoped she'd forget it in the drawer.

She reached for it, pulling it slowly from between the petals. Not giving herself a chance to second-guess, she tore open the flap and unfolded the single sheet inside.

Hello Beautiful.

She smiled, her eyes stinging because she could just hear the sigh Danny always gave when he called her that. Like just seeing her had made his entire day. Her heart clenched, but the feeling wasn't as bittersweet as it used to be.

I have huge hopes you never have to read this note, but...well, if you are, I guess things didn't work out like I planned. Seems to be a theme for us, doesn't it? But don't start feeling guilty. You didn't do anything wrong to me. In fact, you gave me the happiest times in my life and I don't just mean the months we were together. I mean even those days we hung out with what's-his-face, doing dumb things like eating hamburgers and sneaking beers. Loving you made my whole life worth living. Every. Single. Day.

"Oh Danny, if you'd found the right woman for you, she'd have been the luckiest woman alive." Love was such a messy thing. She and Danny were more alike than anything, devoted to a person who couldn't give them what they needed. Miranda ran her fingers over the paper, wishing he could feel it, and kept reading.

I've never regretted it for a second, either, so don't feel bad for me. I've had a great life. My only regret is that I hurt you and I hurt Josh, the last two people in the world I ever wanted to do that to. So, the one who needs to apologize is me, for wanting too much. For asking for something I knew you couldn't give.

I knew what I was getting into, pushing between the two of you. Part of me knew it wouldn't work, but you know me. I had to try. I had to know for myself that we weren't meant to be. I know it now, just like I know that you and Josh were. I'll never understand why it hasn't worked for the two of you yet, but I guess that's one secret I'll never know the answer to.

Well, that and why you love him so much. Seriously, Red. You could do so much better. He's stubborn. Kinda dumb. Did I mention ugly? You've got rotten taste in men, honey. Plus occasionally he's too noble for his own good. You really ought to have beat that out of him by now. You have my permission to take care of it now that I'm gone.

She laughed, probably exactly what he'd hoped. He loved Josh like a brother, no one disputed that, not even Josh. Danny had to know reading his letters after he was gone would hurt. But that was just Danny. As his mother said, always thinking ahead.

So, if I'm in the big firehouse in the sky, I'm going to apologize by asking you to do me a favor. I need you to take care of Josh.

Before you argue that he's able to take care of himself just fine, you know good and well that man can't tie his shoes without you. He loves you. Loves you so much he'd give you up if that's what it took to make you happy. Or at least, if that's what he thinks *will make you happy.*

The underlines beneath "thinks" sort of killed the subtlety of his clue. Well, the man had always been about as subtle as a ball-peen hammer.

He's big on sacrificing himself for the greater good. I'm pretty sure someone with your devious mind can come up with a way to work all of that to your advantage. Get him to see things your way, because he deserves to be happy. And I'm pretty sure if he's with you, if he ever figures out how to show you what everyone else has been able to see since we were kids, you're going to be happy too.

More than my own life, Miranda, I want you both to be happy. If all else fails, tell him he owes you. He'll come around. The rest is up to you, Red. Make it good.

P.S. I left you my car. Josh'll have kittens, so drive it around as much as you can. Something tells me heaven doesn't have action DVDs and I'll need a good show.

Tears slid down her face. The idiot. Trying to play matchmaker from the great beyond. Only Danny.

"Miranda?"

She lifted her head to find Benny standing in the foyer.

"There's a man here from the fire department for you."

She sat up. "Really?" She wanted to ask if it was Josh but excitement clogged her throat. Of course it was. He wouldn't send anyone else. She patted her head, smoothing the curls she hadn't been interested in taming since he'd walked out. Okay, she could do this. Let him do the talking, Penelope had said. Give him a chance to explain himself. Remember that he can't tie his shoes without you. Try not to look so damn happy to see him.

Benny smiled at her, nodding with what she hoped was approval when she finished situating herself on the couch. He turned to the side and beckoned to someone still on the porch.

She waited, listening for familiar boots on the porch steps, a smile on her face as a shadow crossed the threshold and mingled with the long pattern of Benny's on the floor.

Just a few steps and she'd see him. Then everything would be okay again. Just another step...

Chapter Ten

It wasn't Jared.

For two days, Josh had been staring at the evidence spread out in Raul's office and wishing it could have been that easy. They'd closed themselves off, reading files, conferring with the arson investigators and the sheriff. Nothing made any sense.

"How can it not be Jared?" he asked for the hundredth time.

"It could be, I guess." Raul sighed, tossing a file on top of his desk with frustration. "Assuming he's managed to find a way to sneak in and out of Corcoran prison at will."

If only it were that simple.

Neither the flask nor anything else in Josh's house had yielded any fingerprints or help. The sheriff hadn't had any trouble tracking Jared to his cell in prison, where he'd been sent for first-degree manslaughter more than fifteen years ago after he'd accidentally killed his wife in a drunken rage. According to his paperwork, he'd undergone therapy for his drinking and his anger issues. Somehow, Josh couldn't see either problem going away thanks to some handholding in a circle full of other convicted violent offenders. With any luck, Jared would never get out to test himself on the public.

Which meant none of what was happening in Ranch del Cielo made a bit of sense.

He stared at the map on the wall where Raul marked each of the probable arsons from the last year. Looking at them as a whole, the pattern leapt out like a neon sign but it all pointed at the wrong person.

Fire scoured the property where Jared worked long-term as a landscaper. It ate the cabin where Jared would take him in the summers, promising he'd teach him to fish someday instead of just marking property lines and trails for the town. The barn where Danny died was where Jared had worked the year he'd almost managed to dry out and not be such a miserable bastard all the time. Even the boarding house Jared would use whenever Josh's mother managed to throw him out for a night or two. At least four other places stood out in Josh's memory, tied to Jared in some insignificant way or another.

The fires weren't always big. There wasn't a set pattern to the spacing between them. Some seemed purposeful, calculated burns—like the room in the boardinghouse that didn't spread to any other part of the building. Others, though, clouded up like a rage, destroying everything with no trace of rational thought. The explosion at the cabin might have been on purpose...or it could have been inspiration for the car bomb. Almost as if the explosions were fits of anger instead of pegs in a master plan...

"If it's not Jared, it's someone close to him." Josh repeated the conclusion he kept coming back to, but nothing new hit him between the eyes on this pass either.

"Warden's report is that your father doesn't have any significant affiliations. No one from the outside contacts him. No one inside cares about him much either."

"Stop calling him that," Josh muttered absently, turning away from the map. Maybe it was blinding him to something he should be seeing.

"What? Calling him your father? That's what he is."

"No, he's not. Jared is just some bastard I knew once." Knew and tried with every fiber of his being to forget.

"He doesn't seem to think so," Raul replied dryly. "You're listed as his next of kin."

Josh frowned, yanking his gaze from the floor to his friend. "What?"

"His file. Where it says family relationships, there's a listing for son." He reached out his hand to shift through the many manila files stacked there.

"Son. No daughter?"

Raul's hand paused, no doubt remembering. "No, just the one listing."

Josh moved to rifle through another stack. "Why list me? Why not Trisha?" She was the softer touch, his best chance at reconnecting with his family. Josh had occasionally wondered why Jared had never made another attempt to reach them, or at least reach Trisha, who'd spent three days crying after she saw him. Reading the date on the arrest report finally gave him his answer. Jared had been in custody almost to the day of his last visit.

Raul finally pulled it free and flipped it open. Skimming pages, he flipped them over the back of the folder before holding it out. "Yep, here it is. Son. Raymond Sean Whittaker..." His gaze connected with Josh's over the top of the file. "You have a brother?"

"No." Josh grabbed the folder and stared. He hadn't read much of Jared's personal file, preferring to let Raul find the pertinent facts. But this was pretty frickin' pertinent. A brother, eight years younger than himself. Jared hadn't wasted much time after the divorce. Apart from his age and an address in Santa Barbara, there wasn't anything else written about the sibling he'd never imagined could exist.

Raul pushed his chair back to the computer on the table behind the desk. Pulling up a search engine, he typed in the name and waited for something to come up but almost nothing did. A similarly named musician. A link to a widower's support group. Nothing of any import after that.

"Try the mother. She's a victim, she might show up on a database somewhere." Josh watched Raul type in Elaine Whittaker's name, a burning sensation in his gut clenching tighter and tighter as the search engine collected information. Not much more came up, an article about alcohol-related crime, a site with her name in the address, and an image of a woman with a bright smile and a cloud of dark brown hair. "Start with the crime site."

The rundown there was only slightly more detailed than the arrest report. Woman knocked down during an altercation with her drunk husband, accidentally cracked her skull on the hearth of her fireplace and bled out before an ambulance could be summoned. Due to his history of violence and inebriated state at the time of the attack, Jared received twenty years for involuntary manslaughter. Elaine was survived by her parents, Mark and Cara, and her son, Ray...

In other words, bunko.

The second site, though, turned the pain of his stomach into a new kind of agony. Horror.

Pictures of Elaine began filling the webpage, appearing randomly to fill the black space. Happy smiles. Many repeated, cropped closer and closer, as if the designer were desperate to create more images. Many of them showed her playing with or holding a dark haired little boy with sad blue eyes and a careful grin. The clothes were wrong, the environment different, but the face looking back at him was nearly his own at that age. Right down to the inability to let down his guard and enjoy himself out of fear. If that was his brother, the kid clearly suffered from their father's special brand of affection.

Raul scrolled down but the site didn't seem to have any text. Just pictures overlapping each other in a haphazard way, dropping endlessly and pointlessly. Raul moved the mouse over the screen, stopping when it converted into a small white hand. Glancing over to Josh, he clicked.

The screen went black momentarily before a small square of light formed, becoming a movie of a courtroom. Josh recognized the defendant, standing in a worn tan suit, his shoulders slumped, dark hair gone brown and gray.

The judge's voice was scratchy, the film grade choppy, but the canned sound came through clearly when the woman leaned into her mic. "We are here for the sentencing of Jared Whittaker for the crime of involuntary manslaughter in the first degree. Does the defendant have anything to say before sentencing?"

Jared coughed. His voice, when it came, was slow and scratchy, nothing like the deep rumble Josh remembered. "Not really, ma'am. It was an accident, a terrible one that I'll have to live with for the rest of my life. If I could change things, I would. I'd go all the way back to the day I first started drinking and take that back. I'd change it so Elaine never met me. She could have met someone else, had all the kids she really wanted and she would have been happy. I didn't put her first, I never put anyone first, and I should have. Now she's gone. Prison's probably the best place for someone like me. There's nothing out here for me anyway."

"Very well." The judge scribbled on some papers, handed them to her clerk and sighed. "It's a sad fate that a man like yourself, educated and with a child to think of, has come so far that he'd prefer to be in prison. But it's my job to oblige you.

Therefore, Jared Whittaker, you are hereby sentenced to no less than twenty years and no more than the term of your life in the Corcoran State Prison facility." The film jumped, splicing back to Jared's speech, brief as it was, looping. "There's nothing out here for me anyway. Nothing out here. Nothing out here. Nothing out here."

"I think we can safely say we've found our obsessed little firebug. He must think he's avenging his mother by taking away someone Jared cares about in return." Raul rolled the mouse over the loop, but no hidden links waited. He closed the window but Jared's voice continued to play in Josh's head like a mantra.

Raul's theory panged wrong in the wake of it. "Jared would have to care about us for that to work."

"Hey, just because you hate him doesn't mean he hates you," Raul said, a thought Josh didn't like to consider, but couldn't argue. "Maybe the kid knows that." Raul didn't seem to concern himself with the lack of response. "How the hell did he find this film reel? The kid was what, seven, eight, when his mother died? Who would have filmed the trial?"

"Could be news archives. I'm betting something like this was big in Santa Barbara when it happened. What I want to know is how'd he find out so much about Jared that he knew exactly what to burn here to wipe out any trace he existed?" Josh asked. A cold shiver went through him at his own words. A piece of the puzzle slid into place with the sound of steel clanking together in his mind. "I think we have a much bigger problem, Raul."

His friend looked up at him, frowning. "Why? What?"

"The boy. I think he's here to wipe away any trace of Jared Whittaker. That's why he tried to kill Trisha. Why he waited for Miranda to come out of the house. So she'd be close enough to damage the pregnancy. But if he kills us, he's still got himself to deal with."

"You think this little shit is suicidal?" Raul swore richly. "Great, a suicide bomber in Rancho del Cielo. Your family is officially now the most fucked up in town, Josh. I mean that. Sincerely."

Yeah, no shit. But even with that in mind, part of the arson list didn't line up. "Something still doesn't fit. Why kill Danny?"

"Maybe he thought you would be up there." Raul picked up the phone and began dialing.

Maybe... "It's been months. If that's the case and he messed up, he's had all kinds of opportunities to kill me since. But he went after Trisha and Miranda instead. Why?"

Raul began talking, his request to speak to the sheriff registering only slightly as the names began rotating in Josh's head. *Miranda, Trisha, Danny. Miranda, Trisha, Danny. Miranda, Trisha, Danny...* There had to be a reason for attacking them and leaving him alone. A reason to hurt them. The only answer he could conceive was that whoever this kid was, he was trying to inflict pain before he had his grand finale and revealed himself as the one who'd hurt Jared the most.

"Except Jared doesn't care about any of them. It wouldn't mean anything to him if they were gone." *But it would mean everything to me.* He'd have nothing, just like his father. No friend, no family, no wife and no children... "He wants me."

Raul turned his head, the movement sharp, his eyes narrowed.

"He's not out to hurt Jared. He wants to hurt *me*." Danny died because of him. Trisha, broken and burned, because of *him*. Miranda...

"Why you?"

He had to get to Miranda. She was safe, protected, home now according to Penelope, but still, Josh's gut all but screamed at him to get to her. "I have to go. Find out what you can about Raymond."

"What the hell do you think I'm doing?" Raul yelled, but Josh was already running out of the office. "Dammit, Josh!"

Yanking his keys from his pocket, Josh raced to his truck in the parking lot and pulled out with a squeal of tires. Nine minutes to get from the station to Miranda's. That's what she said the official time was. He gunned the engine. Not today.

Senses sharpened to a fever pitch, he swerved around cars, ignored the honking horns and barely made empty intersections by speeding through the yellows at breakneck pace. Sweat beaded on the back of his neck along with a screaming sense that if he didn't hurry, he'd be too late.

This guy didn't want to take Josh on directly. He wanted Josh to hurt. The only target left was Miranda. No one else would ever mean to him what she did and somehow, this kid knew that. He had to know it was only a matter of time until he was found. It wasn't as if he took serious pains to cover his arson. The only time the kid had left was now.

Josh careened onto the long curve of Miranda's street, the sight as familiar as it was nightmarish. Instead of fire trucks and ambulances, there were only neighbors, slowly spilling out of their houses to stare at the flames already devouring the attic of her house while smoke spilled from the upper floor windows like misty waterfalls.

Josh stopped the truck, searching for the officer posted for her security. The green and white car was still parked at the curb, undisturbed. Which meant one thing—Miranda was still inside, her deputy with her.

Without another thought, Josh ran up the porch steps and

into the black smoke awaiting him.

ଓଃ

All it takes is a basket of flowers to get me in the door. A smile. Some professional friendliness. The cop gestures me in, turning his back on me to make sure Miranda is pleased with her present.

She's not. It's almost funny. Her smile dies in degrees. She tries to shore it up, but I'm not stupid. She's inches from bursting into tears. I wonder if Josh knows how much he disappoints her. Does her smile fall like that every time it's not him at her door?

I tighten my grip on the handle sticking out of the basket and give it a yank. Before the cop even realizes something's wrong, it's stuck to the hilt in his lower back. His knees buckle and the guy goes down like a pile of rocks. I pull the knife out, shoving it in one more time beneath the ribs, just to be sure he won't be a problem later. I wipe the blade on his shirt, watching Miranda for any movement.

There's no blood in her face. She's frozen, mouth open, skin like parchment. I doubt her legs could hold her if she tried to get up and run.

"There. Now we should have all the time we'll need."

She keeps her gaze glued to the cop. That works for me. I knock over the flowers and underneath find the things I need. The rope. The flare. The two squeeze bottles of gasoline. I come toward her with the rope, finally getting her attention.

"Who are you?" she asks, numbly. "Really?" Her hand flops almost uselessly as I begin winding the rope around her wrist and the cast.

"You can't tell?" When I was little, it was all my father could do not to call me Josh. Not to mention the resemblance. I broke my nose with a rock on purpose, just so he'd stop. It took more than that to make it happen. "You're the only one to ever ask me that. I figured you'd know better than anyone else."

Her eyes fill with tears. She still doesn't move to stop anything I'm doing. Too afraid to fight for her own life. "Are you going to kill my babies?"

I pull the rope and lead her to her feet. She's not steady. Not clear. A state of shock, probably. Like a lamb to the slaughter, I bring her to the kitchen, to the basement door. When the assignment came to search the house for explosives, it was easy enough to get listed. From there, I could inspect her house from top to bottom with no one having so much as a concern. Set things exactly as I wanted them. Now, I'm pulling her down the wooden steps, listening to them creak as she comes down one single step at a time. Is she trying to slow me down until she gets her answer?

"Yes. I am," I finally answer. Why lie? Even if she fought me, she'd get nowhere. Her destiny is to die here, with me. Nothing will change that.

Nothing.

☙❧

There's a monster in my house. She stared into empty blue eyes. There was no menace there. No hate. She knew his face but she didn't know this stranger watching her. He looked at her, spoke to her, as if she were nothing but a means to an end. He pulled the rope taut. Further down the steps. If she didn't follow, she'd fall and that would be worse. Maybe. *There's a monster in my house...and he wants to kill my babies.*

"Why?" Tears slid down her cheeks, unchecked. "Why are you doing this?"

"Because I have to."

"I don't understand." *Buy time. Keep him talking. Keep him busy.*

"I've been here for a long time, Miranda. And everyone in this town is always willing to gossip, pass a story to pass the time. I know all about you and my brother. I know that he'll do anything for you. And every time something happens to you, every time you get hurt, he hates himself just a little bit more. Imagine how much he'll hate himself when they pull your dead body out of this house. It'll last his whole lifetime. It'll be exactly what he deserves." She ran out of steps to dawdle on. He pulled again, his expression coldly regarding her. He wouldn't be so gentle if she fought him. And she'd get nowhere if she ran. She dragged her feet toward the chair he pointed at in the middle of the dim room. The only light coming in was from the long windows near the ceiling, where Rusty was already sniffing.

She must have taken too long to sit because his hand roughly pushed her down. She gasped when she landed on the seat, a hard lurch to her belly snapping her attention like nothing else could.

"He killed my mother, Miranda," the man continued. He took the rope end and looped it into the lower rung of the chair, then back up toward her. The pull dragged her hands down to the bit of wood seat between her legs. The cast made a clanging noise against it, vibrating painfully up her arm. "He was responsible. If he'd had one human bone in his body, one ounce of forgiveness, she'd be alive. I can never forgive him for that. And now, he'll never be able to forgive himself."

He finished with the knots, backed up to check his handiwork. Miranda stared down too. If she weren't wearing the cast, she might have had a chance, but he knew what he was doing. The lumps of rope were completely binding, and totally out of her limited reach.

"No," she whispered, angry with herself, yanking her hands. They barely moved. The more she tugged, the tighter it got on her wrist. She couldn't let him do this. Meekly let him just end her and her children. She kicked her legs, but he'd tied them to the chair too, and all she could do was shift the chair on the concrete. "*No.*"

Rusty barked at the window, growling. He scratched at the glass, dirt spraying where his paws scratched the ground

"He can bark and scratch all he likes," the man said, almost absently. "He can't get in. He wasn't even smart enough to be concerned when the team came through in force to check the house for explosives."

"He's smart enough to tear you a new ass, you bastard." Miranda wanted to reach out and grab his throat, but all she could do was snarl. And cry. Which was stupid because she wasn't sad. She was angry. Unbelievably angry. "You have no right to be here. Get out of my house. Get out!"

He nodded, his creepy blank eyes not registering the slightest concern that she might get loose. "I'll be gone soon enough, Miranda." Then he turned and went back up the steps.

She yelled after him, but he didn't seem to care. She looked up at the window. Rusty was still scratching, whining now.

"Bark, Rusty. Bark!" *Please God, let someone realize something is wrong.* She didn't hold out a lot of hope, though. Rusty was too well known for barking at the wind. But his excitement had him scratching harder, pushing the window slightly open. She gasped, checking the stairs to see if the man was on his way back. Stupid to call him the man, but what else could she call him? He sure wasn't the baby-faced kid she thought he was. When there was no creaking on the stairs, she scooted the chair closer to the window with a hop. "Bark, baby! Bark!"

Dirt slipped through the crack between the pane and the sill. Just a little more and it would be open. Maybe someone would hear her scream—

The man came down the steps and she closed her mouth, panting from the exertion. He picked up a bag of rocks from the corner and hooked it to one end of a blue nylon rope Miranda didn't recognize. She should, though. It was hanging from her rafter and tucked behind a pipe as if she'd put it there. But she hadn't.

"The inspector didn't know I brought it with me, either," the man said conversationally. "This house is a fucking disaster area, Miranda. It's a miracle it hasn't burned down already." He unlooped it from the nail on the rafter as he spoke, shifting it until it was only a few feet from her chair, kicking the bag of rocks along with it.

Miranda eyed it warily. Just because it had rocks instead of a noose on the end didn't reassure her. He grabbed the slack end and took it to the metal banister. After looping it around, he brought it back to her. His muscles worked easily, pulling the rope tight and lifting the rocks up almost to the ceiling. A jagged knot grew in her stomach as he backed up behind her, then crouched with his arms around her, lowering the rope into her reach.

"Hold out your hands."

Oh God. "No."

"Hold out your hands."

He didn't like repeating himself but there was no way she was going to help him kill her. "I said no."

He twisted his wrist around the rope and held it up with one hand, then used the other to grab her face, his fingers digging painfully into her jaw. "I'm giving you a chance to save your own life, Miranda. That's more than she ever had. Now give me your goddamn hands."

She had to meet his gaze. He was angry that she fought him, but frigid terror told her not to take that rope. He meant to kill her and one way or another, he'd get it done. Closing her eyes, sending a prayer heavenward, she opened her palm away from the casted hand. He slipped the rope between them and watched her fingers grasp it. "Real sporting chance you're giving me with a broken wrist," she snapped, even knowing she shouldn't antagonize him. She couldn't help it.

His lips twisted with what she guessed was his version of a smile. "I never said I'd give you a fair chance. I'm letting go now. Sure you have it?"

"Y-yes." Her knuckles whitened and the rope slipped slightly when he released, but the rocks didn't fall. *Hold on. Don't look at Rusty. Don't let him know there's a chance to get the window open. Hold tight.*

But he didn't go away like she'd hoped. He stayed close, pressing his chest to her arms as he circled completely in front of her. He stared at her, looking for something she couldn't imagine. Then he leaned in, too close. "Now whatever you do, don't let go."

"What? Why would I—" She screamed. He'd put his hands on her shoulders and shoved her backward, letting go when the chair balanced on its rear legs. Real terror coursed through her now, wild and without reason. Her breath came in uneven gasps as she clung desperately to the rope that felt slick in her sweating grip. *There's a monster in my house. There's a monster in my house...*

"There's a stack of bricks behind you." His calm voice cut through the panic. "A hearth, piled about eight inches high. If you let go of the rope, you'll fall and your head should hit the edge hard enough to crack your skull like a melon. I know. I've seen it before."

Oh God, oh God, oh God...

"It won't hurt, Miranda. She didn't feel any pain at all. I watched her until all the blood came out. The second she hit, she was gone. I promise. You won't suffer."

"I'm not...letting go." But her hands already hurt and the rope was nylon. Slippery. Sobs trampled each other to get out of her throat no matter how she tried to hold them in. *Don't let go. Don't let go.*

"Yes, you will. Those rocks are heavy. You're only going to be able to hold them so long. And it's going to get hot in here, because right now, your house is already burning. And behind you, I'm starting another fire. It's not a hearth unless it's lit, right?"

"Don't do this." She didn't want to beg. But pride meant nothing. She didn't want to die. She didn't want her babies to die. "Please, *please*, don't do this."

"It's already done. Except..." He picked up the two small plastic bags. She could see a few broken yard pavers in them He tied them around her elbows, the extra weight making it harder to grip. Soon, it would cut off her circulation, too. He was making sure she fell. Only pretending she'd had a chance. He wanted her death slow. So that when she was found, they'd know they almost could have saved her.

And that would rip the soul right out of Josh for good.

No, she'd hang on. Give him time. He'd come. He always came. If the house was burning, someone would call the station. Nine minutes. She just had to make it for nine more minutes.

He started out of the basement, his duties down there apparently at an end.

"Josh will find you," she yelled his way, eyes on the rope in her fingers. "He'll be here. He won't let this happen. He's never let me down before. He'll be here." She kept repeating the words to herself, a prayer of a different kind. Reassurance to the babies who had no idea what danger they were in. A promise to her heart, for having faith in the man she'd loved and trusted all her life. It was time to trust him *with* her life. "He'll be here."

"Don't you understand yet, Miranda?" The man said from the stairs. "That's exactly what I'm counting on."

☙❧

Josh found the body first. His feet tangled on the big shape and the man groaned. In the smoky darkness, Josh could see that the victim was Benny. Blood slicked the floor beneath them. Turning back to the door, he opened it and carefully lifted the man in a fireman's carry across his shoulders. Before he'd gotten to the foot of the porch, people crowded him, helping him bring the deputy to a patch of grass. Unable to stay, Josh twisted away and ran back inside.

The black smoke choked him as soon as he made it to the living room. "Miranda!"

Was she upstairs? Or down here? She couldn't be conscious. If she were, she'd be outside. "Miranda!"

"You won't find her, Josh." A voice he didn't expect came from behind him.

Spinning, he saw the silhouette standing on the threshold to the kitchen. The light clicked on. "*Andy?*"

"Ray, actually." The kid stepped into the living room holding a heavy sledgehammer Josh recognized from Miranda's back yard. "Expecting someone else?"

Josh stared at him. *Andy?* "You? You've been..." He didn't

even know what words to use. Then the anger hit him, pushing the shock out of his veins. “You tried to kill my sister.”

Andy nodded, remorseless. “She got lucky. But she'll remember me now, won't she? And every time she looks in the mirror, she's going to see what you did to her.”

“You did it, Andy. *You* hurt her.” Josh watched that sledgehammer in Andy's strangely capable looking grip. The sounds of the fire upstairs were getting louder, more dangerous. They didn't have a lot of time before it ate through the support beams. But the kid wasn't shaking. Wasn't unsure as he slowly came closer. He had all the time in the world. Shit, he *was* planning to die in this burning house.

“You did all of this, Josh. Everything. If it weren't for you, she'd be alive. He wouldn't have come home drunk. You. You and your bitch sister. All he needed was for you to forgive him, for you to just fucking *talk* to him, but you couldn't do it, could you?”

“Andy, I don't—”

“My name is Ray!” The sledgehammer swung suddenly, smashing through the small table behind Miranda's couch. “He came home drunk and she tried to leave him. She was tired of being the one he took out all his anger on. Because of you, he hit her. Over and over, until she fell. And she *died*!”

“Ray, I swear, I—”

“You what? You didn't know? You're not responsible?” The sledge swung again, this time at Josh himself. He jumped back, the heavy metal head just missing his ribs. “You think just because you didn't do it yourself, you had no part? Who made you judge? Who gave you the fucking right?”

He charged, leaving Josh no choice but to grab for the long handle and allow Andy to push him into the bookcases. But Andy wasn't in it for the weapon. He let go easily enough, using his rage to begin pummeling him in the ribs. Pain flashed in Josh's eyes as he struggled to shove the maniac off him. But Andy had his hands around Josh's neck, his eyes wild as he tried to squeeze the air right out of him.

Josh dropped the sledge and pulled at the grasping hands. "Where is Miranda?"

"She's dead down there. You took too long. You killed her."

The sick smile so close to his face terrified him. This kid was enjoying this. Josh tightened his hold on the younger man's wrists, pulling at the muscle and bone going slick beneath his grip.

But Andy didn't seem to notice at all. "Just like you got Danny killed. And your sister burned. You know the best part? When I told Randall what I was going to do, that I was going to kill her, even *he* knew it was your fault. And he put up a bigger fight to save her life. You're not half the man he was, so I gave her a chance and you *still* failed." Andy's smile would have stopped his heart if his words hadn't already done the job.

No, if Miranda were dead, he'd know it. He'd feel it.

Every emotion seemed to fill him and when he lifted his fist this time, he brought it down with crushing pressure into his brother's jaw. Again and again, he hit him until all the tension left the younger man's body and Josh staggered forward, hand bloody and his lungs burning from the smoke.

She wasn't dead. She was here somewhere. But where? Where was she? "Miranda!"

A quick glance around showed that the fire had built. The stairs were alight and the heat stifling from above. He strained to hear something, anything, above the sound of wood crackling and fire roaring. He headed toward the kitchen, the back of the house, yelling her name and swiping at the fire dripping down from the ceiling. It seemed to laugh at him, hiding her in its depths. Never before in his life did he hate fire more.

And then he heard it.

The barking that sounded from somewhere... *Down there*, Andy—hell, Ray—had said. Josh moved toward the basement door, not knowing anything, just feeling his way toward the sound. He checked the door for heat and finding it minimal, burst it open. The barking immediately became louder. Rumbling down the stairs, he found Rusty barking at him from Miranda's bound form. Smoke billowed in from the open doorway, but there was enough light to see her lying on her side in front of some sort of makeshift fireplace. Three logs burned almost cheerily compared to the inferno blowing upstairs.

"Josh?" she asked dazedly.

"Yeah, honey, I'm here. I'm gonna get you out of here, I promise, but we need to hurry." Josh looked for some way out other than the way he came in. Wondering how the dog got into the room, he looked up and saw that the small window near the ceiling was open, dirt spread out over a pile of yard pavers on the ground. He followed the line of a blue rope hanging from the rafters but didn't take the time to figure out what it all meant. It wasn't a way out. Rusty must've managed to squeeze his body through, but there was no way either he or Miranda could fit back out.

"Can you get the knots?" Miranda asked, her body still against the concrete. Josh reached for her face, touching her cheek, wishing he had words or the time to say them. Miranda's weak smile was enough for now. "Rusty saved me," she sighed, as if tired. She must have hit her head again when she fell.

"I'm working on it, honey. There's got to be something sharp down here—" A light shone from the stairs.

"Josh, you down here?" Raul yelled over the sound of the house burning.

"Raul! We need your knife!" he roared back. The light came bouncing down the stairs and in a few moments Miranda was free.

"We ain't got much time, man," Raul said roughly. "You carry Miranda. Head for the back door, I think this thing is coming down. Move!" They ran up the steps, Miranda bundled in Raul's slicker and Rusty bringing up the rear. They ran off the back porch, listening to the angry roar of the blaze and the creaking of the over-burdened house.

Breathing in the crisp air and choking on the acrid tastes in their mouths, Josh crushed Miranda to him, hearing her cry in response. Crying he could live with. Crying meant alive. He was even relieved to be feeling Rusty's wet nose. He vowed that dog would never see another day without steak, just for being in that basement when Miranda needed him.

"I knew you'd come for me," Miranda said against his neck as he and Raul moved further and further from the disaster her home had become. With little warning, the upper level collapsed into the bottom floor with a boom. Water overshot the wreckage, but Josh knew nothing could have saved it. Andy or Ray or whoever he was now had wanted it to burn too much. The only chance the crew ever had was damage control.

"Getting to you is what I was born for." He kissed the top of her head, trying to shield her from the sight. He held her close, his legs finally giving way and they collapsed in the grass. "Are you okay? Any pain?" He felt her legs for moisture, thanking God silently that he didn't feel blood. Next he checked her head, feeling for any new injuries.

She shook her head. "When Rusty got in, he knocked the chair sideways. I missed the bricks completely. Is Benny—"

"Paramedics had him when I came in," Raul reassured her, but the look he gave Josh wasn't good. "And before you ask, we found Andy, too. His ass is probably still unconscious. If he's lucky, anyway."

Josh turned his head back to the fire, regret filling him. This was his fault. She'd lost everything, all over again, because of him.

"Don't think it, Josh," Miranda said suddenly, her voice scratchy and raw. "This wasn't your fault. This was Andy. Only Andy."

He wanted to let her absolve him, but he could still hear his brother's pain. Hear the blame that fit so squarely on his shoulders.

"You can't take responsibility for the whole world, Josh. Just yourself. Just your own choices. Andy made his. So did your father. Don't make them victims just so you can be the villain."

"She's right, man. That was one fucked up little nutjob all by himself."

Josh couldn't help it, he laughed. Until he looked up at the smoldering mess again. That would sober anyone. "What about your house?"

It took effort to loosen his hold enough for Miranda to turn her head and look. When she did, she surprised him again by simply watching it burn. "It's okay," she finally said, pain in her voice. But not desolation. She nestled into him. "What matters most is where my home is."

He thought about Danny's letter. He had been trying all his life to make up for mistakes, trying to be worthy of loving her. Of loving anyone. But she'd loved him anyway. The thought of losing her, losing what they should have had... She was right, he had to make the choice to leave the past behind. Or he'd be no different than his brother, hurting others for his own pain. If he couldn't learn his lesson from a sledgehammer, he was dumber than even Miranda claimed.

He kissed her forehead lightly. "It's with me, Rand. No matter what, your home is always with me."

"For better or worse?" she asked, tilting her face up to him.

He stared down, able to see the bruises and the scratches on her cheek. He lifted his hand to caress it, unable to wipe the pain away. But maybe his job wasn't to keep her from being in pain. Maybe his place was to hold her until the pain was gone. It was something to think about. He nodded.

"Death do us part?" As if she needed the affirmation.

If she did, he could give it to her. "Maybe not even then."

"Could the two of you just kiss or something? You're making me sick over here," Raul complained, reaching into his back waistband for his walkie-talkie.

Miranda ignored him. "I'll still drive you crazy. You gotta know that."

"Dispatch, I need a rescue here," Raul continued next to them.

"I like crazy." Redheaded crazy, anyway.

The woman's voice at dispatch responded with a sharp crackle. "Name your emergency, Captain."

"You hate crazy." Miranda chuckled. Her smile probably hurt her face but it kept growing anyway.

"Yeah, Lieutenant Whittaker is seriously screwing up his marriage proposal. The bride is likely to fall asleep or go into labor before he finishes. I might have to take over for him, please advise."

Josh reached over for the walkie. "Lieutenant Whittaker is doing just fine. But Captain Montenga might need assist getting his head out of his ass. Over."

Raul cracked up while Miranda stared at him with huge

eyes.

Josh tossed the walkie back to his friend. "You have to marry me now, Rand. I could get charged for misappropriation of town resources if you don't. Not to mention FCC regulations about language over an open channel—"

She leaned up to kiss him, already laughing.

"Hot damn, dispatch, looks like Lieutenant Whittaker is *finally* getting himself a wife!"

Hooting and hollering could be heard from the other side of the house as personnel began using the other yards to gain access to them.

Miranda pulled away with a colorful curse of her own. "Does this mean I have to go back to the hospital?"

Josh picked her up, shaking his head. Even when the others reached them, he didn't let her go. And when he got her into the ambulance, nodding his head at her insistence that she only planned to get checked out and nothing more, he made room for Rusty on the bench. The EMT almost made a fuss but appeared to decide against it at Josh's pointed look. Miranda only smiled, peaceful and serene as her dog licked her hand. The guy just reached out for the cab doors and pulled them shut.

Yeah, crazy just about said it all.

Epilogue:

"Can you believe it's finally happening?" Miranda looked at her reflection speculatively. Her hair was piled in a cascade of curls upon her head, for once coming off regal instead of insane. The white satin and tulle dress made her look luminescent in the early morning light. At least that was what everyone else said. She thought she looked like the doll topper over a giant roll of toilet paper.

The soft layers of tulle began just under her breasts and supposedly came to knee level. It wasn't like she could see, and she barely remembered what her knees looked like. Although she had gone to great lengths to find a pair of white stockings that would stay up unaided. The sheer material made her feel sexy and attractive, both feelings that had left her several months ago. So what if Josh had been the one to help her shave her legs and rolled them on for her that morning. At least they'd had fun making jokes while they did it.

"It would have happened a lot earlier if *someone* hadn't insisted on Valentine's Day." Trisha came over to stand by Miranda in the mirror. Her own curls were pulled up on top of her head, spiraling down her back. She looked gorgeous in the blood red matron of honor dress. Trisha's recovery had taken time, but Miranda wasn't about to get married without her best friend at her side. Miranda made sure that the dress would be flattering, but would also provide protection from prying eyes by adding a bolero jacket to the knee length satin. RDC might have been wracked by the events of the summer, much of the gossip of late having calmed to a more respectable level, but she didn't want Trisha feeling on display either. The scars on her back were healed, but it would be a while longer before the redness disappeared completely.

"Oh, leave her alone. Every girl wants a romantic wedding and she does only get to do this once." A warm voice from behind them made them turn. "God knows she's waited long enough."

They both smiled as Penelope made her way in with both the flower girls and the veil. She was wearing the second bridesmaid's dress, leaving Miranda to wonder if she would ever be that thin again. The dress hugged Penelope's curves in a way that was nearly scandalous. Without the jacket, the deep cut of the dress's back and the neckline played tug-of-war with Penelope's deeply ingrained classic poise.

Miranda wasn't quite sure which was winning.

Penelope ushered the girls to a sit in a couple of chairs, admonishing them to make sure they didn't stain their dresses on anything. Trisha chuckled, while Penelope's daughter Chloe, who sat with Charlotte hand-in-hand, rolled her eyes.

"Stain them on what, Mom? We're in chairs and there's only a couple minutes till the ceremony. Give me a little credit."

Penelope tsked, but there wasn't much she could say. Pointing a maternally warning finger at the ten-year-old, she turned and held the veil out to Miranda. Both she and Trisha sighed at the long layer of tulle flowing behind a wreath of roses.

"It looks just like a crown." Tears filled Miranda's eyes. Again. The combination of her wedding and her hormones was proving fatal to her make-up.

"Yeah, Cass Hallifax is a genius." Penelope perused the arrangement, tilting it to show them the details. "She has the roses all connected with wire, fitting in all the baby buds and large roses like jewels. It's absolutely gorgeous." The oohing and aahing might have continued longer if Josh and Trisha's mother hadn't stuck her head in the door, declaring it time to begin.

Penelope and Trisha fit the crown onto Miranda's hair, everyone going gooey as they tried fruitlessly to see all three of their reflections in the mirror. With a brief hug, Penelope pulled away and took the flower girls in hand again. Once they were gone, Trisha suddenly jumped back to business.

She handed Miranda her silk purse and took a shaky breath before pasting a determined smile on her lips. "Okay, here we go. Something borrowed?"

"Check, the diamond necklace is Billie's." Miranda touched it just to be sure Josh's mother's pendant was where she left it.

"Something blue?"

"Check, garter, left leg." They'd almost gotten into trouble putting it on at the same time as the stockings.

"Something old?" Trisha asked, oblivious to Miranda's memories.

"Do I count?" Miranda asked, laughing.

"No, but Josh does." They chuckled together.

"Check, my mother's cameo is in the bag. Lucky thing I left it at Josh's before the fire."

Trisha looked her over one more time. "Something new?"

"Check, twins in place." Miranda ran her hand under the curve of her belly to prove it. Penelope had said any day they'd arrive. She just needed that day to wait until tomorrow.

"You're kidding, right?"

"Nope. You can't get anything newer than unborn children."

Trisha shrugged. She knew better than to fight logic.

"Shiny new penny in your shoe?"

Miranda burst out laughing. "I barely got my feet into these suckers. Penny's in my purse."

Trisha didn't seem to see where the penny might fit either, so she let it go. "I guess we're ready."

Miranda nodded. "Could I just have a moment alone?"

"Sure. I'll be back in a minute." A brief hug later and Miranda was alone with her thoughts. She took a deep breath, absently rubbing at her throbbing back. Part of her was sure this day would never come. Another part, the part that had loved even when it seemed hopeless, quivered with anticipation.

"It's finally happening, Danny," she whispered, looking up to the ceiling, wondering if he could hear her. "I know it seems silly, talking to you about this, but I think you'll rest easier now, knowing we'll be okay. Everything's put right now."

Andy—which had turned out to be a legal name change, actually—was getting the help he needed at a mental health facility upstate. They didn't expect him to ever be free, but one could hope he'd find some sort of peace with the nightmare of his childhood. At the very least he'd never hurt anyone else ever again.

Josh still struggled here and there with letting go of the things he couldn't change. But he didn't take it all so personally anymore, either. Progress was slow, but at least it was happening. He and Rusty had even bonded. Right up until Josh took him to the vet to get neutered. But Rusty would forgive him. She hoped.

Raul still hadn't made two bits of progress getting Penelope to talk to him, but one never knew. Hell could freeze over any day now.

All in all, life was pretty good in their tiny place in the world. It would go on, and regardless of what lay ahead, she and Josh would be together. She couldn't imagine asking for more.

It was time. She realized that at this very moment, she had more than she had ever thought to ask for. More than she had ever dreamed possible. She rubbed her belly, feeling it tighten in response. She was more than ready for Josh Whittaker.

Finally, he was ready for her too.

"Wish us luck, Danny." Blowing a kiss with her fingers, she walked out of the room and into the rest of her life.

About the Author

Dee Tenorio is a sick woman. Really sick. She enjoys tormenting herself by writing romantic comedies (preferably with sexy, grumpy heroes and smart-mouthed heroines) and sizzling, steamy romances of various genres spanning dramas with the occasional drop of suspense all the way to erotic romance. But why does that make her sick?

Because she truly seems to enjoy it.

And she has every intention of keeping at it!

If you would like to learn more about Dee and her work, please visit her website at www.deetenorio.com or her blog at www.deetenorio.com/Blog/.

LaVergne, TN USA
02 December 2009
165786LV00006B/106/P